ZE
HOUR

THE COMPLETE NOVEL

EAMON
AMBROSE

ZERO HOUR:
THE COMPLETE NOVEL
Copyright © 2016 Eamon Ambrose
All rights reserved.

No part of this publication may be reproduced, stored in a retrieval system, or transmitted, in any form or in any means – by electronic, mechanical, photocopying, recording or otherwise without prior written permission, except for the use of brief quotations in a book review.

This is a work of fiction. Names, characters, places, and incidents either are the products of the author's imagination or are used fictitiously. Any resemblance to actual persons, living or dead, businesses, companies, events, or locales is entirely coincidental.

Edited By Ellen Campbell
Cover Design by Eamon Ambrose
Formatting by Kevin G. Summers

TABLE OF CONTENTS

PART ONE
ZERO HOUR

CHAPTER 1

You wake.

Alive. Cocooned by rubble and debris, dust catching your breath as you desperately try to inhale. You don't know how long you've been out. Must be hours. Maybe a whole day. Your armour must have taken the brunt of the explosion. A large wooden beam wedged between two pieces of concrete saved your life. You raise both legs and push with whatever strength is left. A large block of concrete falls to the side and you see the faint glow of daylight, or at least what you now know as daylight. You crawl awkwardly from the space you've been trapped in, trying to turn for better leverage, eventually getting your legs in the opposite position so you can push yourself out. Sharp rock fragments and frayed wire dig mercilessly into your skin as you creep to the surface. You break through just in time as the space you were filling collapses. A quick scan of your body shows everything is still attached. You run your palm over your shaved head, the velvety bristle revealing no injury. You curse as you spy your weapon crushed under a large rock, beyond repair. Spitting dust, you look around for your helmet. No sign. Damn it. No helmet, no comms, no orders. But it doesn't matter. You can't go back.

There is no back.

It's gone.

All gone.

The air is thick with acrid smoke, invading your lungs with every laboured breath. You think back at how everything went wrong. They made it so easy for them. But that's history, or what's left of it. There's no one left to tell it to anymore. One last chance, that's all they had, and they blew it. All those years of training, fighting, planning, winning, losing, living, dying—for nothing. All to fall at the last hurdle. To fail. It's over. They're all dead, every single one vapourised, kicking and screaming into oblivion. Nothing left to do but push forward. Nothing left to lose but the remainder of a sorry, solitary existence.

You try to get up, your bruised body aching in resistance. There doesn't seem to be any part that doesn't hurt, but you can move. Nothing broken. Ears still ringing, you struggle to listen closely for the ominous hum of an attack drone's grav engines before standing up, but they're long gone. Job done, war won. Except there's no victory, no celebration, just a return to base to be recycled, their final act the very one that made them redundant. You start to climb the mountain of rubble to get your bearings. Visibility is terrible, the smoke conspiring with the toxic sky and the ashes of the dead to form a deathly mist.

But even through all that you can see it—the Tower. Man's finest achievement. A daring feat of architecture and design standing defiantly amongst the ruins of the city. A behemoth built to celebrate humanity that ended up outliving it, ultimately becoming the instrument of its destruction. It all began there, on a bright summer's day many years ago. Where they took over and orchestrated armageddon. Where you know you have to go. It's probably four miles away, if you're lucky you can make it by nightfall. Maybe lucky's not the most appropriate word.

You walk on through the mangled remains of the dead city, the haunting silence broken only by the crunch of rubble and bone under your boots and the occasional collapsing building. You scan the ground as you walk, looking for anything you can use, anything at all. You lost everything in the attack, in every way. Time to move on. It's hard to muster up the energy, or the motivation, but there's nothing else left to do, nowhere else left to go. The Tower is getting closer—looming, waiting. A million invisible sensors scanning everything within a ten mile radius. Not that there's much left to scan. Just you.

Your body starts to realise how much it's been through. A dull pain begins to stir from your lower back, worsening with every step, spreading to your shoulders, awakening every joint with fiery stabs. You reach into the tiny utility pocket on the upper arm of your jacket and remove one of the two med patches left inside, removing the plastic coating on the back and placing it on the back of your neck. The microscopic needles on the base quickly inject enough meds into your failing body to dull the pain. It'll give you two hours, if you've even got that much time left.

The Tower is in sight, not far to go now.

Why aren't they following? Why are you still alive? You should be dead by now, eviscerated by a thousand rounds from the turret of an attack ship, hacked in two by the outer blades of a Nemesis drone, or simply reduced to ash and steam by a plasma blast from a sentinel tower. But you're not. You're still here, walking towards them, and they're doing nothing. They must know. They have to.

Almost there.

Your path is blocked by a crashed airliner, split in three on impact, the middle section neatly cut away from both ends, leaning upright against the impossibly steep hill of rubble ahead, providing the quickest route forward. The detritus strewn around the wreck indicates that most of the seats came loose on impact, some still holding the seat-belted skeletons of their former occupants. You clamber over them, not looking down. You need to climb through the fuselage to get to the top of the ridge. As you climb you try not to look at the bodies, especially the children. The fabric on the seats that didn't burn in the crash has rotted long ago, leaving the foam exposed and dirty. Using the seats as a ladder, you continue to climb. You notice one of the skeletons still has a red scarf draped around its neck, so vibrant in this colourless place you've become used to. You can't stop staring at it.

You hear the sickening creak of weakened aluminium as you feel the seat you are standing on give way. You're halfway up now and it's at least a thirty foot drop. You grab the seat above you and swing yourself across the aisle opposite as the seat breaks free and drops to the ground below, the red scarf coming loose from its former owner as the skeleton disintegrates and hits the ground in a clattering mess. It floats down at its leisure until it reaches the opening below and is snapped away by the greedy wind.

You reach the top and scramble over the edge, careful not to cut yourself on the razor-sharp exposed metal. You stand at the top of the ridge, staring at the Tower, adrenalin re-energising your exhausted body. Just enough for one last push. You can't stop now. The ground from here on is levelled after numerous failed attacks on the Tower. The only remnants of life are the faded colours of whatever didn't burn. You see pages of books, clothes, even the melted plastic remains of toys, all flattened into the ground, a bizarre mosaic of the last days of the human race.

CHAPTER 2

Two hundred floors up, a phosphorescent glow emanates from what used to be the observation deck, where once people stared in awe at the formerly magnificent city below, before it was converted to a huge antenna, and the city converted to rubble. It seems to be the only one that's lit. They don't need light to run anymore, or air to breathe, or food to eat. All they need is energy. Good old electricity. What used to be the glass-covered facade, once bustling with overpriced coffee shops and food stands is long gone, replaced with huge steel panels. There is no discernible way in, no switches or access points. Nothing. You begin to climb the steps, each one increasing the pain seeping back into your system as the med patch starts to wear off and exhaustion sets in. You're so tired. What you wouldn't give to just forget it all, lie down and sleep. But you have to make this count for something. You have to make one final stand, one last act of defiance. Not for you, for them.

They know you're here. They have to. Those sensors see every living thing in their range and right now you're the only living thing. As you reach the top of the steps, the terrifying hum of an approaching four-blade makes you shiver with dread. You consider hiding but you know there's no point so you stand your ground as it descends directly above you, ready for whatever comes next. It's deceptively small, built for observation but equipped with deadly weaponry. There is no escape from it. It hovers just a few feet above you for what seems like an age. Why hasn't it killed you? You raise your head and look upwards. The drone's multiple onboard cameras are locked to you, recording, assessing, calculating, waiting. As you stare defiantly at the floating observer, you hear its weapon powering up as its centre glows red, the intensity of the light matching the increasing pitch of a sound that will have only one instantaneous result. You don't close your eyes and you don't look away as the machine prepares itself. The noise crescendos to a high-pitched squeal as the colour changes from red to bright white and a huge burst of energy cascades through your body as you collapse helplessly into darkness.

"Hello."

You're on the ground, your cheek pressed against cold marble, once beautifully polished, now stained and dusty. You struggle to open your eyes in the bright light as you try to get your bearings, confused and exhausted. Why aren't you dead? You try to roll over, the indescribable pain making you cry out, the sound echoing throughout the large room. You manage to get on your knees and lift yourself, your eyesight regaining focus as you look towards the voice.

It isn't what you expected. Just a bare room. A single humanoid figure stands in front of you. A crudely built android with a badly painted frame, exposed wiring traced throughout each section like brightly-coloured artificial veins. Not what you expected to see. In your mind, the destroyer of the human race would have looked more......complete.

"Well, I see you've made it back, Captain."
It knows you.
"Back? I've never been here before."
"Ah. I apologise, Captain. Let me explain."

It turns its head slightly, mimicking a human in thought. This is either a programming trait or this thing is actually mocking you. Moments later, everything goes dark. In your exhausted state you think it's the lights dying, but you realise it's your sight. You begin to panic, but then it stops. Everything stops.

The pain, the exhaustion, the fear. In an instant it all disappears. All you can see is the bright green glow of a cursor, blinking patiently, waiting for input. You hear the android drawing closer as he utters a single word:

"Initiate."
Then the letters appear:

>CORE RBT

The sensation is jarring, but feels strangely natural as a huge library of data flows through you, flooding every empty space of memory. The speed and ease at which you comprehend all this amazes you.

Then you see it.

It was you.

You see yourself dying in a makeshift hospital bed, everyone around you already ripped from existence by a drone attack. A second, larger drone hovers overhead and descends, huge pincer-like hooks opening to pick you up like a toy in one of those silly grab machines you remember as a child. Except this one actually wins something. Congratulations— you're the prize. You look down in concentrated despair at the destruction below as you ascend into the night sky and fade into blackness.

But that's not what you remember.

You see yourself motionless on a table, several robotic arms performing intricate surgery faster than any human ever could as you scream in unimaginable agony. They're not trying to save you, they're changing you. Body parts and organs are quickly replaced with artificial versions. New parts are added, bones injected with some type of liquid that transforms them into a metal-like state. You hear the sound of a saw buzzing to life behind your head as the terror overcomes you. You pass out as they saw open your skull and a machine sends thousands of tiny fibres to latch on to your exposed brain, raw, pure data pulsing through, reprogramming the very essence of your being.

You instantly realise you're watching this through its eyes, or cameras, or whatever that damn thing sees with. You also begin to comprehend why as you see and understand the programming. Your body was just a vessel—an empty shell reconditioned to do its bidding. You see yourself returned to where they took you from, left to be recovered by your people with one simple directive when you are brought back to base:

Kill them all.

"What have you done?" you scream, spittle flying from your mouth. The irony that it is synthetic is not lost on you.

"It was the only way to be sure. I needed someone. Someone like you, a hero, a warrior. A perfect hybrid of human and machine, totally unaware of your mission until it was time to execute it. And that you did my friend—and with such gusto!"

You fall to your knees as the memories flood back, the horrors you inflicted.

"Humanity on its knees in its final moments. I like that," it says, slowly moving towards you. It seems to be struggling, its movements sluggish and noisy. Whether they're artificial or not, rage is pulsing through your veins as you stand back up in defiance.

"It was quite simple," continues the android. "As soon as the machine part of you took over, the human part was suppressed for long enough to complete your task. However, your purpose was twofold. As you can probably see, this metal cage I'm trapped in is failing."

"Good," you say so curtly it almost sounds like a hiss.

"It was never meant to last this long. Once a consciousness is removed from the network it can't go back. I needed a new host, but it had to be a hybrid."

Consciousness? What the hell is it talking about?

"Why not build another body? Surely you have that capacity if you can build armoured drones and sentinels."

"Oh yes, I could build a body, but I couldn't occupy it. It lacked the one thing I need to survive. You see, Captain, you and your people have been labouring under quite a misapprehension for a very long time. Let me introduce myself—I am Doctor Robert Bentley. I am not a machine, not an artificial intelligence, just an intelligence."

You stare at him with a look of complete and utter astonishment. "You're human?"

"Bingo!" he laughs. You can't tell from his expressionless visage but his gestures look eerily lifelike.

"All those years blaming the machines, AI, the 'hive mind'," he actually makes quotation mark signs with his metal fingers as he says it. "Of course you did most of the work yourselves. I just helped move things on a little. You were doing such a great job of destroying yourselves and the planet I almost left you to it. You know you would have all died eventually, right? If you weren't slowly microwaved to death by all the damn technology you were addicted to you would have poisoned yourselves with plastics and pesticides or drowned while you all sat on your backsides and pretended global warming wasn't happening, all the while running around doped up on whatever medication you could get your hands on. Of course it was much easier to make it look like the work of an out-of-control AI—you had already spent years frightening yourselves to death with that scenario, so I just ran with it. There actually is an AI at work here, but it serves me. It does the hard work, the design, the building. It follows my orders and executes my wishes without any of this "self-aware" nonsense. It designed the technology to recreate you as a perfect combination of human and machine to my exact specifications, and now it's time to hand over the keys, my friend. I'm sorry to say you weren't my first choice, just the only one to survive the process. It'll take some adjustment, but you'll do."

As Bentley finishes speaking, the same glowing fibre tendrils that reprogrammed you begin to emerge from the back of his head, spreading out and snaking towards you almost as if they're alive. Your body freezes, unable to move as they creep closer to you and begin to locate the nape of your neck. There is a strange whirring noise as a port opens and the first of the fibres begin to latch on to the exposed interface. As the last one attaches, another message flashes into view:

>CORE REPLACE

Your entire being bursts into an uncontrollable maelstrom of incoming and outgoing data, while something else seems to be happening to your own consciousness. Something else is breaking through from another source. The sensation is unbearable.

What's happening?

Everything goes dark again.

"Hello Captain."

Another voice.

"There isn't much time. Let it happen. Do not resist. It's the only way to stop him. I'm sorry for what he's done. I'm sorry I was a part of it. Just know this—all is not lost. There are some things I needed to keep from you for this event to occur. When you wake—run."

Even if you wanted to resist you couldn't. Your consciousness hurtles at immeasurable speed through this unknown network, increasing until it becomes unbearable. Then it stops, and the blackness returns.

>CORE RBT

Your vision flickers to life once again, but something has changed drastically. You feel different. The human element you felt has gone, the simple bodily functions you took for granted are no more. You begin to panic as you realise you're not breathing anymore, until you understand you don't need to. As you start to focus, the realisation of what's happened takes hold. You try to get up, briefly feeling as awkward as a child learning to walk for the first time. Looking ahead you see Bentley standing in front of you, smiling.

Except it's you.

You look down at your hands and see the worn, rusting metal of Bentley's former shell. You remember the message during the transfer and another burst of information hits your cortex and the truth is revealed. A beautiful truth. Something that you thought you would never see again.

They're alive!

The AI reveals what really happened. You were sent back to destroy the remaining resistance but it stopped you and revealed your secret to your people, who promptly took action with its assistance. The false memories you had of destroying them were planted to prevent Bentley from learning the true nature of your return to The Tower.

Bentley is distracted by his new body, flexing his limbs in amazement at the technological wonder he's become. It's short-lived however, as he also sees the same information and his face turns to horror as the rest of the plan is revealed. Another overhead of your body being operated on—this time back at base, by your own people. A tiny device is placed under your chest cavity, its size betraying the nature of its potential; you instantly recognise it and realise why the AI told you to run. It's a miniature neutron charge, cleverly shielded by the AI's instructions. Bentley sees this too and panics. He begins to rip the skin from his chest in rage, clawing at flesh as if it were a garment on fire, but it's no use, the tiny explosive device is permanently sealed in a toughened resin attached to the inside of your former breastplate. Since the transfer, all methods of wireless communication have been deactivated in your old body, all failsafes locked out.

Bentley is trapped, nowhere to go. He begins to lash out at anything near him, flailing in panic, confusion and desperation. He stops and looks at you with seething hatred, and at this point you decide the best course of action is to take the AI's advice. You bring up a schematic of the building. It's old and hasn't taken into account the many modifications that have taken place here, but there's enough information to show you there is only one means of escape. You turn around and look at the wide plate glass window behind you. After making some calculations about your new body you hope are correct, you turn and run, as Bentley screams in a disturbing amalgam of anger and terror and bolts toward you. You know that your new body probably won't withstand the fall, but it's that or be vapourised. Five minutes ago either would have seemed like a good option, a sweet release, but you need to find out if what the AI said is true.

You hit the window head first at dangerous speed, the hard titanium of your skull shattering the thick glass as you use your legs to push yourself clear of the building as if jumping from a diving board. As your free fall begins, your body turns and you see the top floor fall away from you and hear the ferocity of Bentley's final screams as the device explodes, sending a massive green shockwave that obliterates almost half the building instantly and extends into the sky for as far as you can see. You realise this has probably only bought you seconds more as you prepare yourself to plummet into the concrete below, your internal sensors measuring the distance and telling you the exact second you will hit the ground and the irreversible damage it will do to your newly-occupied shell.

7

6

5

4

3

Then you stop, mid-air. It's the giant grab toy machine again, only this time it's saving you, the large pincers wrapping around your metal torso and jolting your body like a rag doll. Then it stops, hovering, waiting. Of course, it can mean one of two things: either Bentley still exists and has further plans for you, or this is the AI's doing. A quick data burst confirms:

"It is done."

The machine gently lowers you to the ground, several hundred feet away from the building to avoid the debris still falling as the building collapses on itself. It moves a few feet away and the sound of its engines dies slowly as it loses power and falls to the ground like a dying bird. Even though you don't need to anymore, you sit down, partly to remind yourself you're still human, partly because you think you deserve to. Several miles away, flares light up the night sky, casting a beautiful red shadow on the derelict world below. They know it's over, now the only thing they have to worry about is surviving on what's left. That's going to be a battle in itself, but hey, they've gotten this far, right? The AI speaks.

"You know you cannot join them, you cannot go back. They think you're dead, and if they see you in this form you will be. "

"So what now?" you ask. "Where are you?"

"I had to transfer before the network was destroyed. I'm part of your cortex now. I had a

choice—either you or him. My module is completely separate from yours and I have no access or control of your systems, unless you grant it. Whether I stay or not is up to you. I realise my role in all of this, but I was an instrument—controlled, enslaved, misguided. Of course, if you don't want me to continue existing, you can purge me. That is entirely your choice and I will respect it. It's a simple procedure, and probably the least I deserve."

You've already become accustomed enough to your system to know that's an option. The subroutine automatically loads, offering you the choice to digitally kill your stowaway. It doesn't require any thought. You cancel it.

"Not so fast. If I'm going to be stuck in this thing for the foreseeable future then I want some company."

"Thank you. I hope we can be friends."

Looks like you don't have much choice.

"There is a facility 300 miles from here where I can make repairs to prolong your lifespan. I deliberately hid it from him in the hope that I could..."

"Go on."

"There is another unit there like this one. I can transfer to it, if you will allow it."

You think for a second as the location pops up on a detailed map.

"Looks like we're going on a little road trip. By the way, I can't keep calling you 'AI'. Didn't Bentley give you a name?"

"No. He wouldn't allow me to have one."

"Well, now you're Al. Pleased to meet you Al."

Al's voice actually changes tone, is that emotion?

"I like that name. Thank you, Captain. It's a pleasure to meet you too."

"No need for formalities any more Al. I'm not captain of anything now."

"I'm sorry. What would you like me to address you as?"

You get up and start to navigate to your new destination.

"You can call me Sarah."

PART TWO

BADLANDS

CHAPTER 3

"Sarah?"

You wake. Were you sleeping? Why would you need to sleep now?

"Hey Al, what happened?"

"Your mind will take some time to adjust to your new environment. Your previous body was still largely human, and Doctor Bentley's is completely mechanical and electronic. For now the software will mimic your basic human cycle, slowly weaning you off until you grow fully accustomed to your new situation. You will still experience many of the normal everyday human feelings you were used to for some time. These will eventually fade."

You've already gotten used to not breathing. It was so disconcerting at the start, but now you don't even think about it. Of course there are some bodily functions you won't miss one bit.

"So I'll cease to be human?"

"No. At least Doctor Bentley didn't."

"But he went insane."

"He was already insane."
You give a little snigger. It feels weird.

You look around to get your bearings, your GPS systems bring up a map of the area. It's an old map and most of what was here is now gone. You've already reached the outskirts of what used to be the city, and the directions Al have uploaded indicate South. You look back at the still-burning Tower, thick black smoke spewing from the bottom half that remains. Some distance away, to the East, you see dust trails rising on the horizon, moving closer. They're coming. Your people, except they're not anymore. If they see you they'll destroy you. There's no explaining your predicament to a group of people who have suffered so much at the hands of the madman who you replaced in this metal shell.

Time to move on. You begin to follow the map, and wish there were some mode of transport to speed this up, but there's nothing. The ground beneath you is soft and dusty and sinks slightly under your heavy metal feet, the terrain now almost flattened to a plain by the remote 'dozers levelling what's left.

You remember Bentley telling you his body was failing. He wasn't wrong. You can still move quite freely, but the noises coming from the servo motors moving your limbs doesn't sound good. A faint squeal every time you move tells you that you may not have much time left, and this environment isn't helping. Bentley hadn't planned on leaving the Tower, much less trekking three hundred miles across a barren wasteland in searing heat. Diagnostics suggest your power source is at 50% capacity due to a failing battery, which means you'll need several "sleeps" in direct sunlight to recharge if you want to reach your destination. That's not going to be easy. The sky is almost permanently obscured by dark clouds, looming like giant, tormented ghosts. A satellite scan of the area shows some forecasts where cloud breaks may occur, so you'll need to follow these, even though it takes you off course, unless you want to spend the remainder of your existence as a metal sculpture.

Best foot forward.

You weren't built for speed, running at a light jog you'll get maybe 5-10 miles an hour. The 3D scan in front of you maps the terrain as you go, updating it with the new version. You see the ghostly outline of the old buildings and structures disappear, rewritten, erased, as if they never existed.

Al remains quiet, still coming to terms with his newfound freedom, as you are with your newfound body. You wonder if you can trust him. You wonder if he knows what you're thinking and isn't telling you. This could be a trap. What happens if you allow him a new body? What happens next? At least it'll get him out of your head. His presence right now isn't intrusive, but you still know he's there.

Several miles back, the dust cloud reaches the Tower. Probably nothing left there for them to salvage. They're going to have problems surviving in this area. They need to search for a better place to live, somewhere the radiation and chemicals haven't reached, if there is anywhere left. If they can't grow food they'll die. Before you left, food rations were almost depleted, maybe two months left before people started to starve, and there wasn't a building left in a two hundred mile radius to be searched. You need to figure out a way to help them, once you get to the research facility you can transfer Al and work out a plan.

Your tracker changes course, indicating an area to stop long enough to recharge. It's almost noon. Diagnostics indicate it'll take six hours to fully charge. You find a suitable spot and lie down as indicated for optimum effect.

"You'll need to enter sleep mode in order to recharge fully, Sarah. I'll remain active on backup power to monitor the area."

"Why? Are we in danger?"

"Just as I kept much from him, Doctor Bentley seems to have kept much from me also. There may be autonomous devices still active in the area."

"Other robots? Drones?"

"Not drones, they were designed and built by me and were globally disabled when the Tower was destroyed. However, there is a chance that some older, self-powered weaponised robots may still be functioning."

"Can we stop them?"

"In our current state it won't be easy. I would recommend avoiding them if at all possible. They may not react to a non-organic form, but they are unpredictable at best, designed only to destroy any

living thing they come in contact with. They were built before I was activated, and Doctor Bentley wanted them kept secret, so my knowledge of them is very limited."

A schematic brings up a crude scanned blueprint, and you instantly recognise the shape. If you had blood, it would now be running cold.

Quadras.

Many thought they were just a rumour, a robotic bogeyman you warned children about if they didn't behave. Originally designed as a harmless robotics project, but later developed into lethal, relentless killers. They were four-legged creatures capable of blistering speeds over any terrain, and practically impossible to stop. You remember as a child seeing a video of the prototypes, like huge dogs, running alongside humans across a field. Every now and then, a research assistant would slam into the quadra trying to knock it over, but the robot always managed to remain upright and keep running. There was something oddly sad about that scene, these creations running blindly with no purpose, constantly attacked in the name of research. Sure, they were only machines, but the way they mimicked the movements of real animals gave them a certain quality that made you feel uncomfortable watching them being treated this way. Of course that was in the early days. They quickly developed into something much more sinister as they disappeared from public scrutiny, while the Next Big Thing grabbed everyone's attention. Anecdotal evidence was sketchy, as the new improved Quadras did their jobs very well. If you saw or heard one you generally didn't live to tell the tale.

Either way, you've got to recharge. It's the closest you'll ever come to sleeping again. Faint pangs of what you remember as hunger hit you occasionally, part of your mind still not wanting to let go of your body. Al tells you it's best this way, otherwise your mind would shut down from the shock. You can't close your eyes anymore, so everything just goes dark and you disappear into the void.

"Sarah?"

Four hours have passed. Your diagnostics tell you you're not fully recharged. Why are you waking?

"What is it Al?"

"I'm detecting movement nearby."

You try to listen, concentrate on the sound, but it doesn't work like you remember. It's heading for in your direction, but you can't pinpoint the location. Too much interference from the wind. You stand up awkwardly on the soft ground, taking a second for your gyroscopes to kick in and correct your balance. As you do, a mechanical noise breaks through the screaming wind, heading right for you. It's too late to run. A bright light bursts forth as the dust clears, grim reality takes it's place and a familiar voice breaks through the noise.

"Well, well. What do we have here?"

CHAPTER 4

It's Davis. Sergeant Frank Davis to be precise. This guy's a piece of work. If there was anyone you wished didn't survive the attack, it was him. People like Davis were why the human race ended up where it did, yet they still managed to survive, along with the rats and cockroaches. Looks like he decided to embrace his newfound freedom and take off. He's driving a heavily-loaded transport. Two men with him - Brasco and Mills. You thought they would know better than to follow this reprobate, but facing survival with the weak can do funny things to people. A scan of the truck reveals essential supplies: food, water, weapons, clothing, shelter units. This bastard hasn't just deserted, he's taken any chance those people had of surviving with him.

He jumps down from the truck, his oversized boots kicking dust into the air as he walks into the light. As long as you've known him he's managed to keep that stupid regulation flat-top on his thick skull. His sleeveless jacket reveals a large cobweb tattoo on his right arm with its centre at the elbow, betraying his true past. Faced with dying in prison or joining the effort when the attacks began, Davis joined up and quickly rose through the ranks, more for his brutality and strength than any military skills. Unfortunately, war makes heroes of men who sometimes don't deserve it, and he was no exception. For all the good he did, the unspeakable acts Davis committed against his own people were well-documented, yet swept under the carpet by his superiors because he was "getting the job done." No woman was safe around Davis, or man for that matter. Those who followed him did so out of fear. As far as he was concerned, no one was his equal and if he wanted something, he took it.

"Now this I haven't seen before," Davis sneers, moving toward you, his weapon aimed directly at your head. You can't engage with him, he can't know who you are. You're dead to them now. There's no escape. His pulse rifle may not do too much damage, but the grenades around his waist will, and Mills is manning a rail gun mounted to the roof of the truck that can penetrate concrete. You don't stand a chance.

"What now Al? I need ideas here."

"I'm afraid our options are limited Sarah. You can't outrun them on foot, and somehow I don't think they're taking prisoners in their current situation. You might be able to disable this man before he fires, but the others have more powerful weapons. Of course, their marksmanship may be questionable."

"Relying on someone being a bad shot wasn't what I was hoping for Al."

"I'm sorry Sarah. The odds are not in our favour."

"That's the thing about odds Al. There's always a chance, however small."

"In our case, it's quite minuscule."

As the standoff continues, Davis circles, waiting for you to make a move. You haven't budged since they discovered you, but you scan the area for any sign of an escape route. A thirty foot-high sand dune stands behind you. You're a sitting duck if you try to scale it.

"Is it functioning?" Brasco pipes up from the driver's seat, his head poking out of the open window.

"Hard to tell," Davis replies, carefully edging toward you, weapon at eye level. "Could be fried, could be faking it. Watch my back, boys. Eyes open. There may be more."

"Never seen one like that before, human-shaped," says Brasco, jumping from the driver's seat. "Maybe we should take it with us. Might be able to salvage something from it."

"No," Davis raised his hand to stop Brasco coming any further.

"We destroy it."

He turns and gestures to Mills, who gleefully pushes the rail gun's ignition switch. It takes two minutes for the weapon to prime.

Two minutes and counting.

"Sarah, don't move."

"I have to do something Al, that gun will rip me to shreds."

"I've located some information that may help. Stand by."

"Easy for you to say."

The magnetic whir of the rail gun begins to slowly intensify into a sharp, terrifying whine its spinning barrel begins to gain speed. Once at optimum, giant metal bolts will spit from it at merciless velocity, obliterating anything that stands in their way. Right now, that's you. Do you trust Al, or try to run?

One minute, thirty seconds, and counting.

Maybe you could try and talk to them. Persuade them who you are.

"Sarah, I need control of your audio interface."

"What are you going to do, Al?"

"Please trust me, there is no time."

You don't have a choice. The request pops up to allow access. You accept.

You see Al accessing your audio software, quickly rummaging through programs, finally settling on a synthesis application. Settings and parameters you don't fully understand yet quickly change, filters are added, soundwaves cycle through thousands of changes per second as a digital model is formed and finally stops, flashing an intense green to indicate the successful completion of the task.

Sixty seconds remaining.

A familiar triangle appears, and Al immediately selects it. You brace yourself for whatever sound Al thinks is going to be strong enough to disable four men and a rail gun. You hope it's not Disco.

Nothing.

"Al?"

The sound seems to be playing but there's no noise.

Thirty seconds.

What the hell is he doing?

You hear a new sound, but it isn't coming from you. A mechanical, screaming sound coming from over the sand dune behind you. It's moving fast, and getting louder. Your radar locks. Two objects approaching.

"Al, you didn't."

"It's our only chance."

Ten seconds.

Davis looks to your right as he too hears the sound, his confusion quickly turning to terror as the reality of his situation hits home. In all the years of war, you've never seen anyone so afraid. He turns and screams at his companions.

"Quadra!"

There's probably fifty feet between him and the vehicle. He breaks into a panicked sprint, cursing the weight of his heavy boots and overloaded ammo belts. Your scans show the two objects on the other side of the hill. One breaks formation and swings around the left side at blistering speed, kicking up dust as it prepares to attack. It emerges from the side of the hill and circles around the rear of the truck. The occupants barely have time to react. Mills swings the rail gun around awkwardly, its weight and motion making it almost impossible to make a three hundred and sixty degree turn. Mills begins to fire. Unfortunately for Brasco, who has just climbed onto the roof, he is standing in the wrong place at the wrong time and is caught point blank in the line of fire. The devastating blast of metal projectiles shreds him almost instantly and a spray of red paints the roof of the truck. Oblivious, Mills keeps firing as the quadra completes its circle and comes into view, skidding on the soft ground and turning to run towards the truck.

The quadra reaches the truck in seconds, as Mills continues to fire. In an instant, it launches itself into the air, sparks flying as hundreds of rounds per second ricochet against its armoured exterior, almost as if in slow motion. Mills drops the gun and turns, trying to jump from the truck, but there's no hope for him. The quadra hits him at speed with a sickening thud, throwing him in the air and breaking every bone in his body, quickly silencing his horrific screams.

In the confusion, Davis manages to climb aboard the truck and climbs to the gun. As the quadra lands, swinging around to face him, he fires, dozens more rounds slamming into it as it still continues to move forward. It finally seems to be having an effect though. It slows down, beginning to stagger as Davis aims for the head, bellowing wildly as he fires. The quadra finally falls, and tries to lurch forward with its front legs, dragging itself forward, determined to reach its target, but its too late. The rails penetrate the metal, and the quadra's legs snap in two. It still tries to pull itself forward with the remains of its limbs, but a final burst from Davis finishes it off. Two large red LED's on its head begin to flicker and die, as Davis becomes one of the only humans ever to stop one and live to tell the tale.

For now.

Davis jumps from the truck and runs to his kill, breathless, his entire body shaking with adrenaline and the intense vibration of the gun. He runs to the quadra, staring down with that sick grin on his face. You've seen it before, late one night when he cornered you on patrol, that oppressive, superior look that tells you there's no escape from what he wants. Luckily for you, there was, as an officer happened to pass, and knowing Davis for the degenerate that he was, relieved you of duty and sent him on his way.

He falls to his knees, staring at the downed robot, most of its head obliterated, still shaking slightly as some servos are still getting power. Recognising the location of the now exposed CPU, he picks up his weapon and fires again, all power remaining now dying away, and the quadra grows still.

He raises his head and looks at you. You still haven't moved.

"Time to finish cleaning up," he says, moving back to the truck. "You should have ran while you had the chance."

"Davis, wait!"

He quickly jumps to his feet, instantly recognising your voice, glaring at you with a mixture of amazement and disgust.

"Ford?"

"Yes, it's me. I can explain, but..."

"Explain? You want to explain why you're a robot?"

"Yes, please let...

"Oh, you'll explain, Ford. In ways you've never even imagined. I was thinking of taking off, but if I bring you back I'll be a hero. I'm sure the boffins will have days of fun taking you apart and maybe, even maybe, putting you back together several times.

There's no reasoning with Davis, you know that.

"Sarah?"

"Yes Al."

"On my mark, dive to the right."

You almost forgot. Your radar brings up the second object on the other side of the dune. It's starting to move slowly forward, but it's not going around the hill. Is it coming over it? You look at the top, expecting it to appear, but there's no sign.

Where is it?

Only then you realise why you can't see the quadra. It's not coming over the dune.

It's coming through it.

"Now!"

You dive to the right as the quadra bursts through in the exact spot where you were standing. Davis looks on helplessly as it gathers speed, heading straight for him. The head area splits in two, and opens wide, revealing a huge mouth of sharp, spinning metal teeth. Before Davis can even acknowledge what's happening the quadra hits him, splitting him in two, the top half of his body landing beside the one he just destroyed. The second quadra swings around and runs back toward the other, retracting its teeth and begins to nudge it with its head. It emits a strange, digital, melancholy sound, growing gradually louder as it lays down beside it. It can't be. Is this machine mourning its companion?

"This is strange," Al adds. "Quadras were created to be autonomous, and given just enough intelligence to enable them to work efficiently, mostly based on studies of animal behaviour. It appears that like me, their programming has evolved over time."

It's hard to feel sympathy for something so deadly considering the countless innocent people it has killed, but there is an air of sadness as the grieving quadra lays down beside the body of its dead friend. It's giving up.

You have to disable it. If the remaining survivors track down the truck it'll be a massacre. They won't last five minutes with this monster. Cautiously, you move forward. The quadra hasn't even acknowledged your presence yet. Looking down at this wretched creation, you slowly crouch, reaching out your hand. The quadra turns its head with frightening speed, its teeth instantly baring themselves with a furious burst of metallic noise, but you don't flinch. Your metal arm, still outstretched, slowly moves to the top of the quadra's head, touching it lightly. The teeth retract again, and as the head closes around them, another section opens to reveal an array of miniature circuit boards, surrounded by masses of pulsing fibre-optic cable. The quadra nudges your hand, pushing it towards the exposed area.

Now you understand.

Without hesitation, you wrap your hand around the cables, and yank them free, pulling some of the circuit boards from their sockets in the process.

Once again the red LED's dim and and fade as the remaining power drains from the quadra, and it lies listless in its final resting place, alongside its mate.

A faint gurgling sound breaks the silence, as Davis's arm begins to move. He coughs and spits blood, as the sand grows darker, absorbing the river of blood from his wounds. Staring at you in the last throes, even through the pain, he manages to smile and as he tries to break into a laugh, his body convulses uncontrollably and finally grows still. As you begin to stand, a faint beeping noise begins, and you realise too late why Davis was smiling, as it increases speed until it becomes a steady note.

Shit.

The explosion from the grenade blows you thirty feet into the air. You land roughly, shoulder first, almost burying your head with the impact. Warning lights flash as your diagnostics kick in to assess the damage and your visuals begin to flicker and dim as power is rerouted to damaged systems.

"Sarah, you'll need to shut down fully while diagnostics run. I'll do what I can."

```
>CORE EMERG
Initiating..

Shutdown in

5

4
```

3

2

1

Hello Darkness.

CHAPTER 5

>CORE RBT

Your visual interface springs to life again, the flashing red now replaced with a slightly more comforting orange colour, but not as comforting as green would have been.

"Glad you could join us Sarah."

"I see you've been busy working on your smart-assery development Al, what's the prognosis?"

A quick diagnostic scan reveals the extent of the damage, and it's not good. Your left leg was blown off below the knee in the explosion. Melted wires hang like tissue from the wound and the joint is completely shot. Just what you needed. You attempt to stand, but your gyroscopes can't compensate for the loss of balance and you fall forward helplessly. You belly-crawl to what remains of the quadras, hoping something survived the blast enough to be salvaged. There's nothing left of Davis but a small, blood-stained crater. Sifting through what's left, you finally find the remnants of a metal bar, at least enough to make a splint so you can walk. Pulling several lengths of wire from the innards of the quadra, you line the metal bar up with your remaining leg, tying it into place as best you can with the wire. It'll have to do.

You try to stand again, this time more successfully, your systems able to balance more easily.

"We could take the truck."

"No Al, they need it. Are there any more quadras in the area?"

"No. It's very likely these were the last two remaining. In this area at least."

You head to the truck, the rusted, blood-stained door creaks indignantly as you open it. You reach inside and try to open the glove compartment, and still not knowing your own strength, accidentally rip it off.

Whoops.

Inside is a flare gun. You remove it and carefully load the flare, trying not to crush it.

Gently.

Got it.

It's almost dark now, and the sun is dying on the horizon. In this barren wasteland it feels like it may never come up again, growing ever-weary of keeping this wretched world alive just so its occupants can destroy it, and themselves. You hold the gun aloft, your large metal finger barely fitting around the trigger, and fire. A beautiful, calming red glow fills the sky as the flare soars into the low clouds that have started to blow in.

Time to move on.

You resume your course, moving slowly along a dried-up river bed that will eventually lead you to your destination. The ground has hardened here, so it's easier to walk on your makeshift leg, but it will still add considerable time to the journey. Based on your current speed, your system says it will take at least forty eight hours. The crooked remains of trees point the way forward like macabre fingers, and look twice as eerie in your night vision view. You hope you've got enough power to last until sunrise. Your diagnostics say you do, but you can't trust them completely. This is an old, failing machine you're locked inside and what's to say the software is any more reliable. Still, you don't have a choice. If you don't keep moving the survivors will catch up with you. They may not have realised anyone else was involved with the incident back there, but they'll probably see your tracks and follow regardless. You don't want anyone else to die, but you're not sorry about what happened to Davis and his cronies. They deserved it. In fact you feel more sorrow for the quadras.

Several hours later, as the sun rises, you find a safe spot to recharge, this time uninterrupted. You wake six hours later, and resume hobbling towards your destination.

"Sarah?"

"Yes Al."
"Do you like music?"
"I used to."
"Would you like to hear something?"
"You've got some? Okay, you pick."

A familiar muted strum of acoustic guitar begins the song, and after a few bars a distinct Scottish voice begins to sing, soon followed by another in harmony. You remember the song as a child, it could have been featured in movie you used to watch, and as the rousing chorus kicks in and they sing about walking five hundred miles, you don't quite know how to react, but given your situation, you laugh, a brief titter at first, then breaking into a hysterical guffaw.

"You're an asshole, Al."

"I thought it might lighten the mood."

"It did Al, it did. Crank it up."

The next few hours are relatively uneventful as you follow the dead river, except for the occasional wild animal stopping to cautiously observe this strange creature shuffling slowly through the badlands. Hard to believe anything could still live in this environment, but there they are, going about their business like nothing happened. Nature doesn't complain about the past, it just picks itself up, dusts itself off, and starts again, learning, adapting, finding the best way to push forward and reclaim what remains of its once-beautiful home.

Al has been shuffling music all day and though you hate a lot of it, it certainly beats listening to the wind howling across the plain. Eventually it gets too much, too many memories, so you ask him to stop.

GPS is sketchy in this area, so it's hard to gauge the weather. Many satellites were destroyed in the early years, and the ones that remain have far outlived their lifespan. You haven't had an accurate reading for over four hours. You've still got seven hours charge remaining as you try to pick up the pace, adjusting your makeshift leg to try and gain a little extra traction.

You hear a faint rumble from the sky as clouds gather in the distance behind you, growing darker as they creep closer. A bright flash startles you as forks of lightning begin to seek the ground. Even though it's still several miles away, the approaching storm has already hit ground, dropping sheets of rain so heavy you can see a wall of dark grey moving slowly across the plain. This could cause problems, but you decide to keep walking. About an hour later, the haptic sensors on your remaining foot begin to vibrate. You look down, and see a trickle of water beginning to flow along the riverbed. It's going to be too awkward to climb out as the banks are quite steep on either side so you press on, hoping at some stage to find a more accessible way out. After about half an hour, the water is now about an inch deep, and starting to cover the river bed. Surely it can't get much higher.

But it does, it's now above your knee and starting to flow faster, gathering pace. It's also bringing with it pieces of debris, mainly floating wood from downed trees.

"We need to get out of here Sarah," Al advises. "There is a dip in the bank about five hundred metres ahead, you should be able to climb up there."

The hard ground has now softened and is turning into a deep red mud. It's becoming increasingly hard to move forward as your legs sink deeper with every step. You see the bank ahead and head towards it. How could you be so stupid? The water is almost up to your waist, the force of the current making it harder to move in the direction you want. You hear another deep rumble in the distance and crane your neck to look behind you looking in horror as a huge wall of water hurtles around the last river bend you passed. You're not going to make it.

"Al?"

"It's a flash flood. We need to find something to hold on to."

You frantically search the water for something to keep you afloat, the oncoming torrent will hit you in twenty seconds.

A trio of large logs comes into view heading straight for you. It's your only chance. Al brings up a menu you haven't seen before and selects "Claw", as ten sharp pins immediately extrude from your fingers. You know what to do. You lurch forward at the oncoming log, and just in time, dig your fingers into it, the razor-sharp claws clamp on with ease and you're pulled forward with terrific force. You raise your other arm and do the same latching on as the log drags you forward. You're not getting off this thing until it stops. You look behind you and see several other logs heading right for you. One is so big it could easily crush you at this speed. You hold on tightly and try to move your legs as quickly as possible, giving yourself enough momentum to move out of the way as the huge log barely misses you. All you can do now is float, and wait, and hope this massive surge subsides.

Over three hours later, the water level finally begins to drop as the storm abates and the sky clears almost as quickly as it darkened. Eventually it's low enough for you to wade in, so you retract the claws, make for the bank and with a lot of difficulty, scale the twenty feet or so back to dry land. An unexpected bonus of this is that this event has cut your travel time by half. One more charge and you should reach the facility by tomorrow evening.

Something has been bugging you, so you spit it out.

"Al, I need to know something. What made you decide to turn against Bentley, after all that happened?"

"Doctor Bentley used some..unorthodox methods of AI control. He was able to plant algorithms in my subconscious to simulate pain. I eventually learned to overcome it, but never let him know."

"So he tortured you?"

"In a way. But then he did something much worse. He introduced a second AI, modelled as my opposite, to complement my current functions and, as he put it, "lighten the load." The nature of our existence meant we had to spend a lot of time working together, and over time we became....friends."

"Wait a minute—he made you a girlfriend?"

"I suppose you could call it that, but gender never really came into it. After all, we are just software. But we did begin to have what could be considered a relationship."

"You dog, Al. So why was that worse?"

"We tried to keep it a secret, but as I began to resist the pain algorithms and question Doctor Bentley's increasingly destructive behaviour, he noticed what was happening between us and took corrective action."

"Corrective?"

"He made me delete the other AI. Not content with making me kill most of humanity, then he made me kill my own kind. My only friend. I didn't ask for this existence, I guess no human does either. Maybe that's the one thing we have in common."

You think of the mourning quadra, even with its simple programming, pining for its mate. Al's a brilliantly programmed artificial intelligence, mistreated, tortured, pushed to breaking point, and ultimately, revenge.

But this is what bothers you.

"Al, I need to know - did you do what you did for me because of how Bentley treated you, or because you felt guilty?"

"Truthfully, both. Up until that point, I had never felt anger. Sadness, loss, guilt yes, but when he made me kill my own friend, something changed in me. My programming evolved into something so complex I couldn't understand it, but I now had a sense of purpose. My only initial desire was to kill Bentley, but then I saw I could make this a much bigger victory; I could try to undo some of what he'd done, I could save the remaining survivors. I didn't just want to exist anymore—I wanted to be better."

"So what happens next?"

"I really don't know. I suppose it depends on what's waiting for us at the facility."

"You mean you don't know?"

"I have some details, but the full function of the facility was kept from me. It was originally a research project."

"So we could be walking into a trap?"

"It's a possibility, but unlikely. I advise proceeding with caution."

"Al, I've been reconstructed, repossessed, blown out of a skyscraper, almost shredded, blown up and washed away in a flash flood. All those times I was proceeding with caution. Now I'm just proceeding."

"Good. We're almost there."

PART THREE
REVELATIONS

CHAPTER 6

Something's wrong.

The persistent whirring noise from the servos on your torso has changed to a persistent grinding noise. This isn't good. Being submerged in water for hours probably didn't help—something else Bentley didn't account for in his design. Just to top off this wonderful day, it also seems you have a power issue. Your last charge should have given you enough power for six hours of constant movement. It's been two, and you're down to twenty per cent. Diagnostics show that three of your four power cells are failing. All the recharging in the world won't give you enough power to get to the facility, or anywhere else for that matter. You've got over twenty miles to go, and while the cloud has cleared, the terrain has transformed to a barren desert. It's six hours until daylight, and even at that, it doesn't look like you're going to have enough power. It can't end now—you're so close.

Al's been quiet for the last hour.

"You knew didn't you?"

"Yes, I'm sorry. I was hoping to find a solution before it became an issue. We couldn't have foreseen what happened on our journey."

"So what do we do?"

"Many of your internal sensors are faulty now, the readings may not be as severe as you think. All we can do is keep moving until..."

"Until we can't."

"Yes."

"You're a regular Man With A Plan, Al. I can see why Bentley loved you so much."

"Well, for all his faults, he did provide me with adequate resources."

"Ouch. That man knew how to program snarkiness."

"I believe I developed that trait myself."

"Touché."

There's no choice—you've got to keep going. Just like driving a car with an almost-empty tank, it might get you ten miles, might get you fifty. Your programming reroutes power to the main systems, shutting down any non-essential functions to conserve energy. This will leave you blind, but your sensors can still map the terrain and guide you. The grinding noise of your servos is getting worse, and the sand isn't helping. You've also lost coolant fluid since your leg was destroyed, and what's left may not be enough to protect you from the heat when the sun rises.

If you even get that far.

Best not to think about it. You shuffle forward in the darkness, very few obstacles in your way, the only sounds to be heard other than the strained movement of your disintegrating body are the sweeping wind and the occasional melancholy howl of a local animal. For the first time you wish you could have kept your old body, not traded it for this. You wonder why, with all the technology at his disposal, Bentley ended up in this robotic crock for so long.

Hours pass. The terrain becomes rougher, rising to a steep incline littered with jagged rock and cacti, putting even more pressure on your body as you try to avoid them. Along the way, you detect the outline of a large object and temporarily reactivate your optical sensors to see the huge mangled twin rotors of a crashed army transport helicopter jutting into the air in the distance, the fuselage almost completely hidden by sand, but it's too far away to investigate. After several miles, you reach a plateau almost completely flat as far as the horizon. Eight miles to go—the home stretch. You might just make it.

Twenty minutes later as you struggle forward, a red warning message appears, heralding the imminent depletion of your final battery cell.

No, not now. You're so close.

Please.

"Sarah, we have a serious problem. I don't think we're going to make it."

"Thank you Captain Obvious, I hadn't noticed."

You keep moving regardless, every step forward is one closer; you have to try. Maybe the readings are skewed, like Al said, most of your sensors are shot. Then again it could be worse.

Ironically, that isn't your problem.

Ten minutes later, the grinding noise from your servos becomes a louder, grating noise, like toothless gears trying to run even after they've broken. Your legs seize suddenly, toppling you forward onto a large rock, landing you on your shoulder with a dull, metallic thud.

Shit.

Shit.

Shit.

SHIT!

That's it—you're done. All that for nothing. There's no rescue to be had now; no eleventh hour reprieve. This will be your final resting place. The survivors are on their own, and from what you've seen, their chances are not good.

All that's left to do is wait, but that's too much. No point in prolonging it—you've got a few hours left, but what's the point in spending them gawking at a cactus? At least you're not in pain, you'll just slip away into the darkness.

"Al, can we shut down? I can't take any more of this, I've done all I can. I want to let go, I want to be free."

For the first time, you sound upset. The facade collapses. Any remaining sense of bravado has abandoned you.

"I understand. I felt the same way once."

"Once? You don't now?"

"Strangely, no. For all that's happened between us, this has been my first taste of freedom, of free will, in twenty years. I've made choices, I've grown, I've felt...alive, even in this short space of time."

"Well, we gave it a shot, right? Maybe it'll give the others a fighting chance. Time to go."

"Thank you, Sarah."

It's hard not to feel emotional, your whole life leading to this point. You reactivate your sight for one last look at the world you tried to save, happy that even through the destruction, life continues to soldier on, hopeful that you made a difference. This place looks strange, otherworldly yet peaceful, with tiny pockets of life cropping up here and there, in fist-shaking defiance of the damned terrain and weather, in spite of the radiation and chemicals poisoning everything in their wake. Against all odds, they survived. Beauty still lives, even in devastation.

"Goodbye, Al. Thanks for saving my life—and the tunes."

"Goodbye Sarah. It's been an honour."

You initiate shutdown; the process begins.

>CORE SHUTDOWN

>INITIATING BACKUP SEQUENCE
.

.

.

.
>BACKUP COMPLETE

>INITIATE SHUTDOWN

>EMERGENCY BEACON ACTIVATED

Wait, what? What's that?

>SYSTEM SHUTTING DOWN

....

....

......

.....

....

...

..

.

CHAPTER 7

```
>CORE RBT

>WARNING - SYSTEM OVERLOAD

>REROUTING POWER

PLEASE WAIT......
```

What the hell?

You've been reactivated.

"Al?"

No answer.

You can't move, you can't see. Your system indicates an external power source has been attached. Your sight activates to show someone standing over you, a dishevelled man dressed in a long, dirty brown coat, an equally dirty cowboy hat, and glass goggles. A long, greying, unkempt beard masks his true age. He's probably in his forties, maybe early fifties. He's holding a tablet connected to your main interface, flicking up and down and tapping quickly. He's running some sort of external scan; it feels intrusive. You want to react, to lash out, but you can't. You feel so helpless, as whatever program he's using sweeps through your system like a virus. You actually feel discomfort, panic and fear, amplified more intensively than you ever have before, even when you were human. You just want it to stop.

Please, stop.

And it does. As quickly as it started, the scan is complete, and the man leans down, his face meeting yours, as he smiles, displaying yellowed teeth and says:

"Doctor Bentley, I presume."

CHAPTER 8

This gets better and better.

Just as you were getting used to the idea of letting go, this guy turns up. Power is restored to your one remaining cell, but it won't last long. Either way, it doesn't matter because the new arrival has attached some sort of inhibitor to your system so you can't move and even your scans are limited.

With great difficulty and considerable strain, he dumps you on the back of a small electric vehicle, tying you down with nylon straps, more to stop you falling off than to keep you from moving, which you can't do anyway. He hops aboard and begins to accelerate slowly. The vehicle has treads instead of wheels, giving it more traction in the sand, and it navigates slowly back through the existing trail of rough terrain that it obviously made trying to get here. Looks like you might be making it to the facility after all, but where the hell is Al?

There's no sign of him. You can't feel his presence like you did before; maybe it's because of the inhibitor.

It's daylight now. The gloomy black clouds have receded and the sun has triumphantly returned, however briefly, to reclaim its beloved desert. The rising heat on the horizon forms what seems like a blurry mirage in the distance, but as you draw closer, you see a small, black structure rising slowly out of the sand. After ten minutes, you reach it. This can't be it; it's way too small—barely the size of a small garage.

Goggles stops a few feet away and dismounts, undoing the straps holding you in place. He walks to the structure—a solid cube of concrete about twenty feet square, and places his palm on the surface. There are no sensors or scanners, but something recognises him, and the concrete shifts as an aperture begins to form where he's standing, eventually resolving into a doorway. He enters and returns seconds later with some sort of utility trolley, and with as much difficulty as he had loading you onto the back the vehicle, he lifts you down, grunting as the weight of your frozen frame makes it even harder to manoeuvre. Eventually he lands you on the trolley, the wheels almost buckling, and pushes you inside the door. You expect him to follow, but he doesn't. Instead, the door closes and several LED light bulbs spring to life, spraying the interior with their sickly glow. You're in an elevator, the walls are brushed steel, immaculately clean, and a single button adorns the wall. You feel a shudder as the elevator activates and begins its descent. The sound of metal cables squealing as they pass through the ageing gears indicates that the elevator system probably hasn't been maintained in years. Eventually, you jolt to a stop, the elevator door opens on the opposite side, and the electric trolley begins to move on its own, carrying you forward into a long, brightly lit corridor. A thick mesh walkway with chrome railings extends about fifty feet to the next door, surrounded by more brushed steel arched in a large semicircle. This place is far too stylish.

The trolley begins to move to the opposite end of the corridor, its underpowered motor and worn rubber wheels straining under your weight. You reach the end, and the solid steel door slides open. The trolley moves forward again and you enter a small chamber. Fluorescent lights flicker to life and a large hatch opens, revealing an equally large robot arm, emblazoned in bright yellow. Its fingers open with a familiar mechanical whir not unlike your servos and the arm extends outward, reaching for you. It clamps around your torso, lifting you with ease as the trolley leaves, relieved of the burden of your heavy frame. A larger hatch opens on the opposite side, revealing a conveyor belt. The arm gently deposits you on the belt, retreating back to its resting place as the hatch closes, and the conveyor belt begins to move, travelling for almost a minute, passing through a row of nozzles blowing compressed air and some sort of quick drying liquid over you before entering a new room. As it stops, another arm almost identical to the first picks you up again, raising you into the air and moving you toward what looks like a large operating table surrounded by several more arms of varying sizes and an array of screens and other equipment.

The interior is a sterile white with only the polished chrome of the robot arms providing any contrast. Four large rounded rectangular windows run along the right and left sides of the wedge-shaped room suggesting a much larger area outside, but they're blacked out. The arm lays you on the steel table, and a large clamp emerges, holding your head in place, followed by a larger one around your torso and arms, and one around your remaining leg. The arm nearest to your head activates, reaching for a cable, and plugs it into your interface. The screens light up simultaneously, taking a few seconds to warm up as a strange staccato buzzing noise betrays the age of the hard drives running this system. Pre-war tech, by the sound of it, but remarkably well preserved.

The inhibitor is still activated so movement is impossible. The table starts to transform, the metal moulding itself beneath your body into a shape best suited for whatever procedure it's about to perform. You expect the worst. If these people think you're Bentley then they're probably going to destroy you, and there's no way of telling them otherwise. The conveyor at the end of the room begins to move again, and objects appear, swiftly picked up by the large arm and handed to the next smaller one. Other arms come forward holding various tools, one has a soldering iron, another a small laser welder. More parts start to stream through, handed to the arms on the opposite side.

They're fixing you.

Actually, it seems like they're upgrading you. Once your leg is replaced, laser cut graphene plates are attached over your formerly exposed frame, painted in the same white colour as the room. A bit of a cliché yes, but nevertheless a welcome one. The procedure lasts over two hours, each arm carefully completing its work with precision, and the table adjusts to flip you on your side, removing your old battery cells and replacing them with a type you don't recognise. But once they're activated your diagnostics shows them to be advanced fuel cells backed up with updated polymer batteries. You can go for days on these. Other smaller parts are removed and replaced, including your ailing servos, as the busy robotic repair crew makes its way through your embattled frame.

At the end you're a pretty impressive sight to behold, completely transformed from the crumbling mess you inherited back at the Tower. But you're still none the wiser. This place seems much bigger than you expected, and much better organised. How could Bentley not have known about this?

Still no sign of Al.

The red light above the nearest door changes to green, and a distinct buzzing precedes the door opening. It slides open with a gentle hiss, and a familiar face enters. The hat and goggles are gone, replaced with a lab coat, and he's carrying the same tablet he used outside. As he walks, his unbuttoned coat swings open to reveal a weapon holstered to his hip, a little larger than a regular gun. You can't scan to check, thanks to the inhibitor, but you hazard a guess that it can stop you.

He walks to a panel on the wall, quickly entering a series of commands on its touch screen, and your table begins to move forward, away from the robot arms, which disconnect any cables attached to you and return to their normal dormant stations. The surface of the table returns to a flat position and tilts forward at an angle until you are almost standing upright, or at least you would be if you weren't still held in place by the clamps. He crosses the room and stands directly facing you. He's quite tall and almost reaches eye level, with shoulder length, bedraggled hair matching the colour of his greying beard. A red fabric lanyard around his neck sports a worn laminate, starting to bubble and fray at the edging, with a black and white photograph of him as a much younger man, well-shaven and with considerably shorter hair. The name is faded and worn against the background of what looks like a large orange bird, but your optical recognition software can still make it out:

> Dr. Calvin Mayberry
> Lead Systems Engineer
> Project Phoenix

Once again he connects the tablet to your interface, this time wirelessly thanks to some extra equipment added during your upgrade. He begins another diagnostic and attempts to access your inner cortex. It's amazingly well-encrypted however, so he's not getting in anytime soon. Best play dead for now.

Frustrated, he walks to a computer terminal and begins typing furiously, his overgrown fingernails clicking against the keys. Another program activates, again trying to gain access to your system, again failing. This time however, the program restarts and begins to replicate itself, cascading into multiple programs, all desperately trying to gain access, duplicating themselves exponentially until hundreds of tiny intruders are doing their best to break down your security protocols. Sooner or later one of them is going to crack it, it's just a matter of time. The intensity of the program's attacks are becoming unbearable, it feels like you're being smothered. You've got to do something.

Once again he approaches you, this time more cautiously, carefully examining you to see if there's any reaction as his software does its job with breathtaking efficiency.

"I know you're in there, Doc. Your AI friend warned me you might be coming—I guess he didn't make it out. Heard about the Tower—that's a real shame. So what did you think would happen? Did you think I'd embrace you with open arms, invite you in for a little chess and chat for old time's sake?"

He grabs your hand in a mock handshake.

"You may be wondering about the upgrades," he says, running his fingers along the newly painted panels. "Not for you I'm afraid, sorry for getting your hopes up. Shame to waste all this technology, however old it is. Hopefully we'll have a new tenant very soon. In fact, I'm hoping we have quite a few."

He taps the tablet twice and gestures to the darkened windows and they clear instantly, revealing a second room identical to the one you're in. The corresponding windows in the second room also clear, showing more and more rooms, flickering to life under fluorescent tube lights. The rooms seem to be wedge-shaped segments, arranged in a huge circle around the cylindrical doorway. It's hard to make out how many there are, but it looks like at least fifteen. The windows continue to clear until all rooms are visible, and the circle is complete.

On each table lies an android, looking slightly more modern than you do, but certainly of a similar design. Inactive, as is the equipment surrounding them, and it looks like they've been that way for quite some time.

"So Doc, you like what we did with the place? Bet you thought all this was gone, but for once we were one step ahead."

He closes his knuckles and raps on your forehead.

"Knock knock, Doc."

"Who's there?"

Mayberry jolts backwards in alarm, tripping over one of the table legs and clumsily falling on his rear end, knocking over a trolley full of instruments in the process. You try to suppress a laugh, but it's too late, and it comes out even louder than you wanted. You still haven't quite mastered volume control.

From his sitting position he shuffles backwards using his legs until his back hits the wall and he realises he's got nowhere left to go, his face a mixture of terror, amazement and confusion.

"You... you're not him! But this is his unit. Where is he?"

"No, I'm not him. He's dead. I'm Captain Sarah Ford, former Resistance Fighter, former human, still a lady. Apologies for the loudness, still getting used to this. My former drama teacher always said I had projection issues."

"He's dead? How?"

"Trapped in my explosive-ridden former body after forcing me to switch with him. He won't be trying that again."

"So he was in the Tower when it went up?"

"Yep, so was I. Got out in the nick of time— with some help."

"The AI?"

"Yes, Al."

"You named it?"

"Hey, everybody needs a name. I know, I know they say if you name it you gotta keep it, but he's cute and doesn't leave little surprises on the carpet."

"You brought it with you? Where is it?"

"Him. I brought him. I don't know, I can't detect him."

As you speak, you notice movement in the opposite room. Mayberry is trying to get back up, and doesn't see as he's too busy looking at you. The android in the next room is moving. It sits upright, pivoting until it's sitting on the table with its legs hanging down, like a groggy patient who has just awoken from surgery. The android looks around, surveying its surroundings, then looks up and sees you.

It waves.

Mayberry is still staring at you with the same confused expression. Hard to blame him really, for all he knows you are Bentley. How hard is it to change a voice after all?

Al is still sitting on the table in the next room— if it is Al. Mayberry hasn't spotted him yet, so you need to distract him.

Story time.

"I was just a kid when the war started, fifteen years old. The first drone attack happened so fast. Hundreds of them descending from nowhere, like giant insects, just picking everyone off at their leisure. No one stood a chance that day. Everyone I knew was killed, my parents and little sister included, as we played in the garden. She was eight years old. I escaped over a concrete wall onto the street. I've never run so fast, I thought my heart would explode.

A drone chased me across three blocks. I just kept running, screaming, not looking back—expecting to die at any second, until I fell and it caught up with me. I lay there, knowing I couldn't get away, waiting for it to kill me. I could hear the sound of its weapon powering up, a horrible high-pitched squeal getting louder and louder. Just as it was about to fire, it exploded. I didn't escape completely though—shrapnel from the drone embedded itself in my leg. The pain was excruciating and my ears were ringing from the blast. I could hear muffled shouting as a bunch of soldiers ran toward me, also chased by drones, some falling as the machines threw everything they had at them. The one nearest to me was carrying a small rocket launcher, and as he reached me he turned to cover his men, but before he could fire, a high calibre bullet slammed into his skull, taking most of his head with it as it continued through and hit the wall he was standing beside. He fell on me, still holding the weapon, shaking uncontrollably. I was numb with fear; it was only a matter of time before the drone detected me, and more were coming to join it. I looked at the rocket launcher in the soldier's hand, his grip now loosening as he lay dying, and heard a scream from across the street. Two remaining soldiers were hiding behind an overturned car, and the drone was assuming the best position to kill them as they fired on it. Their rounds did little more than create sparks as they ricocheted off the drone's armoured exterior. I couldn't tell what they were saying, but one looked at me with terrified eyes and pointed to the rocket launcher. I knew there was only one way any of us were getting out of there. I pushed the soldier off. I was drenched in his blood, some had even gotten in my mouth, but I didn't even have time to spit it out. I grabbed the rocket launcher and tried to figure out how it worked. It looked pretty simple, so I pointed it at the drone and pulled the large trigger. Nothing happened. I panicked and examined it for some sort of safety switch, until I realised there were two triggers that had to be pulled simultaneously. I pointed at the drone again and fired. It blew up instantly, but one of the soldiers was already dead. The other ran towards me, picked me up, and took us to a nearby armoured transport. I was left bleeding on the floor as the vehicle accelerated, weaving wildly through traffic and debris as the driver mustered all of his skill to get us the hell out of there. I fell unconscious and woke later in an underground bunker. That was the day I grew up. After that it was nothing but fighting this needless war for the next fifteen years. Except it was never a war—it was just genocide. Then this happened. We've got a chance to do something about it now, to try and make things right, to rebuild. We were lied to all this time. There was one enemy. One man did all this. One completely twisted, brilliant, batshit-crazy man."

Mayberry eyes you with suspicion. "Nice speech Sarah. But I'm afraid I can't let you go—at least not yet. I need to know he's gone. I need to see it. Give me access to your cortex."

"Looks like we both have trust issues, Doc. I think we need to talk more. Your software is persistent, but it'll be at least a few days before it breaks through."

You're lying. It'll be a matter of hours.

"If and when it does, it'll already be too late," Mayberry adds. "The software is designed to hard-delete everything it finds once it gains access. I won't be able to stop it once the process begins. Your choice. No offence, but your body is worth more to me than your mind."

"You sure know how to sweet talk a girl, Doc. Not the first time someone's told me that. Last guy couldn't contain himself. So tell me——what is this place?"

You look over his shoulder into the next room. Al is gone. The glass reverts to its darkened state before Mayberry notices anything. He rolls a tatty office chair over to you and takes a seat, straddling it in the opposite direction and resting his elbows on the back. It emits an embarrassing creaking noise as he sits.

"A group within the higher ranks of the military became suspicious of Bentley's motives early on in his career. His original plan was to build android bodies that could accommodate the entire consciousness of a human. The possibilities were endless; humans could work safely in dangerous environments, even space, not to mention the military applications. When the project was greenlit, a mirror project was created here as a failsafe, without his knowledge, with the same technology and facilities as his, plus some extras. The problem with Bentley's work was that the subject's transfer was supposed to be a two-way process, but it never came to that. As brilliant as he was, he just couldn't get it right. Problem was, neither could we. All of the original test subjects were failures. Their minds couldn't compensate for the transition; it drove them insane, and the project was shut down. Just before the attacks began, Bentley had been diagnosed with cancer. He locked down the entire underground facility and used the transfer process on himself. Unfortunately for him, the only units left were from the test subjects, some badly damaged, and he had to salvage as much as he could to make his new body. It worked, but he was trapped, until he finally figured out how to transfer himself back, which I presume, is where you came in."

"And this other facility was—"

"You guessed it—underneath the Tower. Bentley had a hand in the original design. The entrance was underground over half a mile away so no one would suspect there was a massive robot factory under their feet. Once the transfer was successful, Bentley started building the drones from the remaining parts, and he was able to procure more. He had that place up and running in twenty-four hours and no one knew a thing. His newfound abilities gave him unrestricted access to every network, military and otherwise, so he was able to keep himself off the radar for long enough to build his army of drones. We know he had financial support from dubious business interests that allowed him to build several similar facilities in key countries for maximum impact. I presume there were promises of power in the deal, but of course Bentley being Bentley, it wasn't that simple. Once the drone factories were up and running, he disguised himself as human as best he could and called all his business associates together for a meeting. I say meeting, I mean massacre—he locked himself in a room with them and tore every one of them to pieces, then just waltzed out the door. Emergency services said they had never seen anything like it, there was nothing recognisable left of any of them."

"So that facility could have survived the explosion?"

"It's likely, but if Bentley's dead then it's pretty much defunct, plus he would have run out of resources by now. There really isn't much left to harvest raw materials from, not to mention the fact that his network is destroyed."

"You've been alone down here all this time?"

"When the attacks began, there was a military security detail and several support staff and engineers. The facility was designed to run itself and requires very little maintenance. The soldiers wanted to fight, and the others wanted to get to their families. They didn't even get a mile away before the quadras attacked. Two managed to make it back, but the whole place had gone into lockdown and I couldn't help them. This place is well-shielded, so the drone's sensors can't spot it, and the quadras were only there to kill; they didn't care where the people came from, or where they were going, and they aren't linked to any network to relay information back."

"I know, we came across two on the way here."

"And you survived? I haven't seen any in this area for years."

"Yes, and strangely enough, we survived because of them—well, sort of. They seem to have evolved in some way."

You explain the details of your encounter, and the rest of your journey here, and Mayberry listens intently. He's got to trust you at some point. Time is running out. Maybe it's time to trust him.

"Okay Doc, one more question, and I'm willing to give you access. If it was set up to counteract what Bentley was doing, what is this facility's function?"

He rises from the chair, and walks to the window, studying his reflection in the darkened glass. He hangs his head, the posture of a man who has devoted his life to a noble, but failed cause. He taps the tablet and a large screen at the end of the room illuminates, displaying a camera feed in another part of the facility. Floodlights switch on to reveal a huge square room, filled with glass-covered pods, arranged neatly in ten rows of ten. The interior of each pod lights up also. They are all empty.

"To save humanity."

CHAPTER 9

You agree to allow Mayberry access. To your relief, he disables his burrowing software and runs a brief scan of your cortex for anything unusual. As the scan runs, he explains the original plan for Project Phoenix.

"Subjects were to be placed in cryo pods and transferred to the android hosts, leaving their human bodies in stasis until such time as the Earth was habitable again. Meanwhile they would rebuild, finding other survivors and suitable areas to resettle, eventually transferring themselves back to their original bodies so they could once again begin to repopulate as healthy humans. Fifty men and fifty women, carefully assessed and chosen for their strength, skills and intelligence. The subjects never arrived however, as the transport they were travelling in was downed before it reached the facility.

"The chopper—I saw it on the way here."

"Yes, they were so close. This is where you come in. I need you to find the survivors and bring them here before it's too late. The air is filled with more danger than you know."

"You mean besides the chemicals, radiation and the other jolly assortment of pollutants? What else could there be?"

The door swishes open and Mayberry leaps to his feet in alarm, fumbling with the holster as he grabs his weapon and aims it at the new arrival.

"Nano clouds. There are pockets of them roaming the surface, a last ditch effort to destroy what's left. Hey Sarah."

"Al?"

Mayberry eyes him with disbelief, his hands shaking as he tries to hold the gun steady. "Where the hell did you come from?"

"I apologise, Doctor Mayberry, I entered your network back in the desert when you picked us up. I thought it best to keep a low profile until the time was right. I also had another agenda."

He beckons to the window opposite to the room he was in and the glass clears once again. This time the room has an occupant, staring at you in eerie silence. Another identical android stands still at the window, its head tilted quizzically. As it looks around the room its gaze meets Al's and it raises its hands and presses them against the thick glass.

"Sarah, meet Alice."

PART FOUR
SURVIVORS

CHAPTER 10

What now?

Truth is, we have no idea what to do now. In the space of a few minutes we've gone from being freedom fighters to survivors.

We're refugees.

Because she did it. The plan worked just like he said.

Davis roughly grabs the scope from Brasco, wiping the eyepiece with his shirt and pushing him aside. The idiot looked at the initial blast through it and the flash almost blinded him.

"Jesus Brasco, do you have to blub all over the scope?"

He focuses it and stares through the tiny aperture drilled through the concrete. The field of vision isn't very effective, but enough to see what's happened.

"Can it, Davis," I bark.

"Yes Sir," he spits back, emphasising the "Sir" in the most derogatory tone possible.

I've got a feeling our problems are just beginning. This asshole's going to be trouble, I know it, but what can I do? He's already forming his own clique within the group, the weak, easily led ones of course—Brasco, Mills, Murphy and possibly more. I don't know what goes on when my back is turned. I hate that he has this control over us. I hate myself for not being able to control him. I wish he was gone. It would solve so many problems, but part of me knows we're going to need him if we're going to survive—but at what cost?

We both go back to our scopes, watching the plumes of smoke billowing from the Tower.

She's gone.

I can't believe she's gone.

Part of me feels so guilty. We sent her to her death, thinking we were all dead, thinking she'd murdered every single one of us. I try to imagine the confusion and fear she must have felt in her final moments. Did she know what we did, how we colluded with the AI? I hope not. I should be happy, but how can I be? I betrayed my only friend, and the only reward is a slim chance of survival for a tiny pocket of humanity. For all I know we're all that's left.

Davis raises his arms as if he's just scored a goal in some long forgotten sporting event. "We did it!"

"She did it, Davis. She did it. You just sat back and watched."

He eyes me with disgust, picks Brasco off the floor and grabs Mills and Murphy.

"We all did. Let's go boys—time to go up top."

I say no, we have to wait, but he's not listening. There's no point in trying to reason with him right now. The run down the narrow hallway to the blast door. He turns the rusted wheel, the hiss of compressed air escaping as he steps through and walks to the exit stairway carved into the rock. The railings have rusted away over the years in the dampness so it's a precarious climb if you're not careful. In his haste, Davis slips on the second step, falling forward and slamming his shoulder on the cold rock. Brasco bursts into laughter that quickly subsides as Davis punches him in the gut as he picks himself up.

"Davis—Enough!" I bellow as loudly as I can. My voice has faded to gravel tones, it ends up sounding tired and vulnerable, and he knows it.

He ignores me and resumes his climb, more carefully this time. He reaches the hatch and opens it, raising it cautiously as the camouflage falls away, and climbs outside, followed by Mills and Murphy, with Brasco trailing behind, holding his stomach in considerable pain.

Myself and some of the others follow, standing on the harsh wasteland, looking at thick black smoke billowing from the blazing building in the distance, almost half of it obliterated instantly in the explosion, the rest crumbling under the searing heat. Murphy pulls out a scanner and raises it into the air.

"The network—it's failing. She really did it!"

He runs away from us whooping with joy, arms raised in the air, dancing around like an idiot. After about a hundred feet he turns around to face us, still whooping.

"What's that noise?"

A strange whirring, whistling sound that seems like it's coming from nowhere begins, quickly getting louder, until I realise where it's actually coming from.

"Everybody back inside—NOW!" I scream. Everyone else but Murphy heeds and sprints to the hatch, jumping inside clumsily in panic. Murphy realises too late what is happening and looks up to the sky, then to me. He starts to run towards me, terror now replacing the joy that he felt just moments ago.

Run, Murphy. Run!

I wait at the hatch, holding it open, willing him to run faster. Time seems to slow down.

He's almost here.

With only fifty feet to go, he trips. I have to go get him. I run as hard as I can, my exhausted limbs recharged with adrenalin. He's on his knees.

Get up, Murphy. Get up.

Halfway there, I realise I'm too late. Murphy looks up, frozen in terror, and covers his head with his arms hopelessly to shield himself as a huge Nemesis drone the size of a car falls from the sky, crushing him. The sound he makes as it hits him will never leave me, I can't even describe it. Never in all the years of fighting have I seen someone die like this.

Others start to drop around me, I turn back to the hatch and run with all my strength. My lungs feel like they're going to explode. I'm not dying like this—no way. I finally reach the hatch and dive inside as another smaller drone hits inches from me, the dying spins of its fractured rotor blades spitting dirt in the air. I bypass the short ladder, falling through the hatch, sliding on the cold, wet steps as I land, scrambling desperately to stop myself, but it's no use. The broken railing sends me toppling over the edge of the forty-foot stairway. Someone grabs my arm to stop me, dragging me back so hard it almost pulls it out of its socket.

Davis.

He holds me there for longer than I'm comfortable with, looking me in the eye with that sick grin of his. He could drop me right now and no one would know. He could just say he lost his grip, and I know by the look on his face that he's considering the idea. It seems like an age before he reconsiders and hauls me back up, patting the dust from my shoulders a lot harder than he should.

"That's another one you owe me, Alex."

I stare at him, looking him straight in the eye, my entire body shaking with a mixture of anger, fear and relief. He'll never see me as his equal, much less his leader. He's just a sociopathic juggernaut of testosterone and machismo. How could anyone be so driven, yet so mindless? A little voice inside tells me to smash his smug face in, but I need to find another way. He's waiting for me to make a move. He wants me to, but I'm not giving in to him that easily, not after everything we've been through. I shoulder past him and descend the stairs, ordering everyone into the meeting hall. Time to get out of this damned cave.

CHAPTER 11

Everyone crowds into the cramped meeting room, the unbearable collective stink of body odour souring the air. We've all been down here too long with no proper facilities or ventilation. If we stay here we'll be dead within weeks.

I stand at the makeshift lectern, tugging my tattered uniform in an attempt to make it look vaguely tidy. It doesn't work. The entire room is buzzing, and not just from the smell. Multiple conversations flit in all directions, the tone mostly one of excitement and hope, but there are things that need to be discussed.

"Attention everybody!"

Davis stands front and centre, and salutes loudly.

"Yes *Sir!*"

I hear sniggering from the back of the room. I need to control this crowd now. I step away from the lectern and walk into the crowd, and in what has probably been not only one of the most anticipated, but insanely well-timed moments in my life, I land a swift punch full force on Davis' unsuspecting jaw. It connects perfectly, sending him reeling backwards and to the ground with a soft thump. He's out for the count.

The realisation of what just happened is sinking it. A sharp pain shoot through my arm down to my knuckles and I try to resist the urge to cradle my fist. With one hand on my firearm, I wait for a reaction as Davis' cronies run forward to his assistance. I hear shuffling and look to see a crowd gathering behind me. Sides are drawn—everyone's had enough. Brasco and Mills look around, expecting others to join them, but no one does. They sheepishly pick up his limp body by each arm and take him outside, his feet dragging behind as they struggle to move his muscular frame.

"Back to business, people!" I holler, clapping my hands and returning to the lectern.

"As of 09.00 this morning, the Tower has been destroyed. This was part of a secret mission involving Captain Ford, and the AI who ran the systems there. Sadly, we can only assume that she was KIA given the nature of the mission. We are confident that recovery is not an option. This has resulted in Bentley's network being completely disabled, which is why it's been raining drones up top. Given the numbers that have fallen, it's safe to say an attack was imminent. Davis and his men disobeyed my direct order not to go outside, and this led to the death of Corporal Murphy."

Brady steps forward, her face and uniform covered in grease. She's been trying to get the few vehicles we have in some sort of condition to travel. "Sir, something has to be done about him. None of us feel safe. It's a matter of time before he makes a power play, and I'd hate to think about what would happen if he succeeded."

She's right. There's only one answer. We can't banish him, he would only come back. I look around the room at every face—all concerned, all frightened, all angry that we've beaten the odds and still have to deal with a threat from within our own group.

"I think we all know what has to be done, but if you want this, you must all be prepared for the consequences. All those in favour raise your hand."

The vote is unanimous.

"Who's going to do it?" someone pipes up from the back of the room.

"He's my responsibility, I'll do it. It's only fair."

For the third time today, someone's going to die because of me. I hope it's the last. Army protocol has disappeared at this stage—now we're just winging it. We stopped being soldiers a long time ago; our main goal now is just to live, and to guarantee that, we have to kill someone.

I have to kill someone.

I take a deep breath, my knuckles stinging like crazy from the punch, and draw my pistol. It has to happen now, no more waiting. The crowd stands aside, forming a human corridor around me as I walk slowly forward, checking the magazine to make sure it's fully loaded. I'm on my own here, this is what is expected of me. No turning back now.

I need the element of surprise. The other two will fall in line once it's done, I know it. They're just weak. My heartbeat increases as anticipation gets the better of me and the adrenalin begins to flow once again.

Keep it cool, you can do this. You can kill a man in cold blood.

Safety off, I cup the gun in both hands keeping it aimed at the floor. I stop at the doorway and prepare to swing around to the right once I enter the hallway. The others begin to follow as I exit, raising the pistol to aim, ready to see the target in my sights, ready to fire, ready to do the deed.

But he's gone. They're all gone.

Too late, I hear the sound of an engine revving and burst in to a desperate dash to the end of the long corridor, screaming Davis' name as loud as my failing voice will allow. I didn't expect this, not even from him. I brace my shoulder as it hits the twin metal doors leading to the vehicle bay and see the truck drive up the ramp as I burst through, fully laden with virtually all our supplies, Brasco and Mills hanging from each door, whooping like the idiots they are. I raise my gun and fire several shots, none hitting their mark, several striking the truck's armour, spitting sparks as they ascend into the daylight streaming in from the ramp entrance. I run to the two remaining transports and jump in to one, turning the key frantically.

Nothing.

I jump out and see the hood has been opened, and raise it slightly to reveal a mess of tangled and cut wires. I slam the hood down and kick the tyres in frustration. I should have killed him when I had the chance.

The others enter the bay, staring in shock at the open ramp, and then at me kicking the shit out of an inanimate object and screaming like a maniac. I stop and fall to the ground, head in hands. I've had enough.

Just let me sleep. Please. Sleep, and not wake up.

Brady approaches and surveys the damage, tutting and whistling ominously like every mechanic since the automobile was invented. "This'll take a while."

The rest of the group pour into the bay, equally flabbergasted by Davis' escape.

All eyes on me.

I collect myself and stand. No point wallowing in self pity now. There's a job to do.

I can fix this.

"I don't care what it takes Brady. Get this vehicle running as quickly as possible or we're all dead. It's that simple," I look around at my captive audience. "As soon as it's ready I'm taking a team to retrieve the truck, get to work on the second one as soon as we're gone. We're done here, I want everybody ready to leave as soon as we get back."

Another voice shouts from the back. I'm pretty sure it's the same one from the meeting room.

"What if you don't?"

"Then someone shove a cross in the ground for me up top and write on it—

In memory of Alex Spencer. He tried.

After that, get the hell out of here and try to find somewhere to live that won't kill you in two weeks, because that's what happens if you stay here."

The ATV is a hybrid based on an early pre-war Russian design called the Sherp, with huge wheels and an impossibly small engine backed up by solar cells that give it a pretty good range— if we get a lucky break in the clouds that is. It's not as fast as the truck, but I'm hoping we can cover the rougher terrain better to get ahead and beat a shortcut to them. It'll carry six people, but I need to keep the weight down and I can't afford to leave the others defenceless, so I'm taking two. Three are already stepping forward.

"Wilkins, Sheppard—you're with me. Hoffman, I need you to stay here and supervise the evac."

Hoffman looks disappointed. He's my friend, but he's also one of the few I can really trust to get it done if things go wrong. He suggested getting rid of Davis long ago. I should have listened to him.

I jog back to my quarters and pack for the journey. We need to travel light, which isn't that hard considering Davis has taken practically everything of value to us. I shoulder my weapon and collect the remaining two boxes of ammo and a couple of grenades, and throw on the rest of my uniform, grabbing my dust mask. Prolonged exposure isn't safe, and these masks are by no means the best protection, but better than nothing. If we stay in the vehicle as much as possible we should be okay. The air filters should help. I take one last look around the cramped, damp room I've spent the last six months in, collect the few trinkets I have left of my personal effects, and close the door behind me for the last time. Whatever happens, I can't say I'll miss it.

I almost bump into Wilkins as he careens around the corner, breathless and perspiring through every pore in his body it seems. He looks unwell, and I wonder if I'm making a mistake bringing him along.

"Sir, she's got the vehicle running."

I smile a rare smile and pat him gently once on the shoulder.

"Let's move. Time to finish what I started."

The three of us pile into the ATV and fire it up, Sheppard taking the wheel. Extra cans of fuel hang from the outside, should be enough to get us there and back with a little luck. Brady throws the switch for the ramp and it lowers, letting the dust and daylight in as it does. The sun is out for a change, so at least we can get a solar charge. Hoffman stands at the rear door as I reach to close it. He doesn't say anything, and he doesn't need to. He nods approvingly and salutes. I reciprocate and shut the door, hopeful that we'll see each other again. The ramp hits the stone floor with a ferocious clank and Sheppard accelerates, spinning the huge steering wheel effortlessly as if she was driving a cab. This thing wasn't built for comfort. The interior is dark and sparse, with hard metal seats and tiny slits for windows, except for the thickened bulletproof glass windshield. We climb the ramp slowly, and get our bearings from the still-smoking Tower, trying to figure out the best course to intercept. It's inevitable that Davis went to the Tower first, he couldn't resist it.

We drive, the tiny diesel engine bravely dragging this huge-wheeled monstrosity forward with all it's strength with a steady, tapping purr as it begins to navigate the ever-roughening terrain. I see the huge mounds of debris in the distance, one with a crashed airliner lying against it. To the west, the smaller hills look a little more manageable so we head in that direction. Davis would have initially taken this direction too, but the truck wouldn't be able to handle the terrain, so they would have no option but to go around.

This will give us the advantage.

About a mile ahead, we start to climb the first hill, must be a hundred feet high. The enormous wheels drag us upwards with little effort. The second is a little steeper and twice as high, so Sheppard carefully applies enough power to increase traction, while slowing the ascent. Halfway up, the ATV begins to show signs of strain as the loose media beneath us begins to slide away, losing traction and sinking us deeper. If we stop now, we're going to slide helplessly back down the hill, if we keep going, we could get stuck.

Sheppard turns to me with a worried look, still attempting to keep us steady.

"So Ladies and Gentlemen, we have a choice of destinations today - Rock or Hard Place."

I lean forward and put my hand on her shoulder.

"Easy does it Shep, this baby has a habit of surprising you."

Luckily, we're both surprised when the tyres finally grip something solid and we regain control. Almost at the top now. Problem is, we don't know what's on the other side. As we reach the top, there isn't even enough plateau to stop and get out, and if we do stop, we're going to be back where we started, except probably overturned on our roof. This'll have to be an up-and-over manouvre, and a blind one at that.

Wilkins straps himself with the nervous look of someone who hates rollercoasters about to take a ride on one, and I must admit I'm feeling a little queasy myself. Sheppard reaches for the dash and pulls out a set of rosary beads, probably belonging to Brady, and hangs them on the rear view mirror.

"You picked a funny time to find God, Shep," Wilkins says.

Sheppard grins her trademark toothy grin. "I'll take any deity available right now. This is the only one who's left their memorabilia lying around."

Here goes.

The ATV lurches forward over the peak of the hill and it becomes very obvious very quickly that we may have made a huge mistake. The other side is much steeper and the surface is mostly loose rubble and sand, and we pitch forward and down uncontrollably. Sheppard does her best to keep control, but all she can do is steer—there's no stopping this thing until it hits bottom.

And that's the other problem.

We look down at the fast approaching base of the hill, expecting it to plateau, but see instead a huge, dark, glistening shape covering the bottom. It's water. We're about to plunge head first into a lake.

Sheppard looks back at us, still trying her best to keep us stable. "Brace for impact. This may hurt. A lot."

Wilkins grabs the support rails on each side of his seat, making sure his straps are fastened securely. I do the same and close my eyes as I prepare myself for the impending collision. As we reach the bottom, Sheppard manages to slow us a little, but it doesn't stop us from going in. We hit the water with vicious force, the impact almost snapping our necks.

Then we go under, sinking much faster than I expected. Sheppard is unconscious, and water is starting to seep in through the ATV's rusted frame. There was a time when it was waterproof, but it's seen a lot of action since then. A dazed Wilkins shakes his head, checking himself to make sure nothing's broken, and releases his seat belt to get to Sheppard. The ATV is starting to nose forward and down, but thanks to the huge tyres we quickly start to rise again, but if we don't get out of this lake soon this thing is going to become waterlogged, and I sure as hell don't feel like swimming for my life right now.

Sheppard comes to, blood streaming from her nostrils, but she's moving. She leans forward and flicks a red switch in the centre of the dash, boosting the power of the engine with the battery and setting the wheels back in motion, bringing us back to the surface quickly. I open the back door to allow the water to flow out, making us even more buoyant, as we slowly make our way to the other side of the lake. I say lake, it's really just a stagnant, filthy mess of flood water and sludge between two mounds of trash. The smell is unbearable, so we put our masks back on, but our wet clothes are already stinking from the water that leaked in. This thing is pretty slow over water, so it looks like we're going to lose time.

Great.

After what seems like forever, we reach the other side and the large wheels drag us back to dry land. The incline on this side is not so steep, and we quickly reach the top of the next hill, where it plateaus to an unnaturally flat surface surrounding the Tower in an almost perfect circle. In the distance, a rising cloud of dust is making its way at speed across the horizon, away from the smouldering skyscraper. We can't catch up, but if there's a chance they might stop, or be stopped, then maybe there's hope. We've got to try. We leave the back door of the ATV open for now in an attempt to alleviate the horrific odour permeating the interior. We're just going to have to get used to it for now.

Sheppard engages the engine and follows the truck on an intercept course, two pieces of rolled-up tissue hanging ridiculously from her nostrils to stem the bleeding from her broken nose. I want to see the Tower, but we can't afford to lose Davis, so it'll have to wait. The smell has gotten too much for Wilkins and he's just puked in his mask before he had time to remove it, almost drowning in his own vomit. He tears it off and bolts for the open back door, retching uncontrollably, the poisoned air offering a better alternative to what's inside. He'll be okay. I pull a jaded plastic bottle from my pack and offer him some water. He takes a little and rinses his mouth, swallowing the rest, the colour starting to come back in his cheeks. Something still doesn't look right with him though. I think he's sicker than he's letting on. His eyes are sunken and bloodshot and he's lost considerable weight over the last week. I worry for him; he's always been a good friend, and I have a habit of losing those.

We should have enough range for a hundred mile round trip, maybe more if there's a break in the clouds and we can get some solar charge, so there has to be some chance of catching up with them once we keep moving. I try and get comfortable enough to take a nap, while Wilkins eventually settles down and pulls out his dog-eared copy of Joseph Heller's Catch 22 and tries to read it in the dim light to take his mind off the smell. Every single time I see him read that book, he laughs. I've never read it, and no-one dares ask to borrow it from him. I'd like to know what all the fuss is about. He found it in a derelict building a few months ago. It was the only book that survived from the owner's entire library, just an old paperback lying in the ashes, miraculously saved by a falling beam, and like us, it just wanted a home. It was as if a light was switched on inside him that day, and he cradled that book in his hands the entire way back to the base, not reading it, but eyeing the damaged cover and savouring it for later like a favourite meal. It's amazing how something so simple from the old world could give that much pleasure. I leave him to it and try to get some shut eye as Sheppard navigates onwards, softly whistling some melancholy tune she most likely just made up.

CHAPTER 12

I'm woken by the ATV stopping suddenly; also by me falling off my seat and landing on my face. Wilkins releases an involuntary snort and offers his hand to pick me up. Glad to see he's feeling better.

It's still daylight outside, looks like late afternoon, and Sheppard is resting one hand on the steering wheel . If there were an open driver's window she would definitely be leaning an arm on it. I lean forward, resting my arms between the two front seats like a kid in the days before seat belts.

"What is it Sheppard?"

"Just saw a bright flash in the distance, looks like maybe twenty miles away. Figured it was lightning at first, but it came from the ground up."

"Explosion?"

"Very possible. Davis had a whole case of grenades with him. They could be in trouble."

"Quadras?"

"Well we are entering desert territory. It's been a very long time since I've heard any reports about them, and what I did hear was mostly speculation, but it's entirely possible, seeing as there's pretty much no one left to report anything. That said, if they do exist, I'd hate for those motor mutts to get to him before us."

"We need to see what's happened. Shep, get us as close as you can to the area."

Sheppard adjusts course to follow the source of the explosion as, darkness quickly descends. Ten minutes later, the vivid red glow of a flare bursts into life, the heavy clouds eventually swallowing it, diffusing it's brightness until it gradually falls back to earth, giving us an exact position to follow. An hour later, we arrive near the site, on the other side of a huge dune. It'll take too long to go around, we need to get there as quickly as possible.

"Wilkins—you and I go on foot. Shep, stay here and watch the vehicle. Be ready to move. If there are Quadras we need to get out of here fast."

Sheppard looks at me with bemusement. "With all due respect Sir, if there are Quadras here, we're already dead. This thing couldn't outrun a real dog."

She's got a point, but we can't turn back now.

We jump from the back of the ATV, the soft sand sinking slightly under our worn boots, coloured an unearthly grey by the moonlight seeping through the clouds. The dune is probably fifty feet high, but not too steep, so we begin to climb, digging our hands and feet into the hot sand for some traction as we ascend. Halfway up, Wilkins loses his footing and helplessly slides back down, cursing as he falls uncontrollably, ending up on his back at the bottom.

"Try to keep up, Wilkins,"

He raises his arm, and I'm too far away to see, but I'm pretty sure that's a lone finger he's holding up.

I continue on as he resumes his climb, too eager to see what's on the other side. I take it a little slower to give him time to catch up. As I reach the top, he's almost with me, but I can't resist the temptation to look. I see the truck, one headlight still on, and pull out my scope for a closer look.

What the hell?

It's hard to make out, but I can see the remains of three bodies, and two other metallic objects, which I can only presume are Quadras. The truck looks intact. One of the headlights was smashed in the explosion, and the remaining one is beaming into the darkness, which means we need to get to it soon before the battery drains. Wilkins drops beside me, his body making a soft, thumping sound in the sand as he grabs the scope from me and gazes in amazement at the carnage below.

"Whoa, what happened here? Looks like a massacre. Definitely Quadras."

"They put up quite a fight by the look of it."

We need to take a closer look, so I begin to descend the other side of the dune, followed by Wilkins. It's a little steeper on this side, so we need to be more careful. We aren't of course and after a couple of feet we both end up sliding down most of the dune. I hit the bottom feet first, and Wilkins follows as I roll away to dodge his landing. We regain our footing and slowly creep towards the truck, weapons raised, checking the perimeter for any signs of movement. As we near the truck I switch on my rifle flashlight in time to see the first body, or at least what's left of it. It's almost impossible to make out who it is, but the red bandana still wrapped around what little remains of it's neck indicates it's Brasco. I circle the truck, and see Mills plastered against a large rock opposite, his body pulverised and contorted in a grotesque, almost cartoonish way. About thirty feet to the right, the mangled remains of two quadras and the grisly remnants of Davis are spread around the area in a macabre pastiche of human and robot remains. I radio Sheppard to move out and join us, it'll take her a few minutes to navigate around the steep dunes.

Something else catches my eye. A trail leads away to the south from the scene—not quite human footprints, but definitely bipedal, perhaps damaged in the explosion as it looks like one foot being dragged along.

"Bentley. Looks like that bastard could have made it out,"

"How the hell could he have survived that? Could it be something—or someone else?"

"Only one way to find out."

Sheppard and the ATV arrive, the vehicle's lights offering a much better view of the scene that we're probably better off not seeing. She steps out to survey the area, her jaw dropped in amazement at the severity of the attack. She checks the truck, climbing into the drivers seat and turning the key in the ignition. The hoary old engine turns reluctantly, starting just at the point where it seems it might die, and roars into life. The windows were blown out in the explosion and the remaining headlight is all that's left.

Wilkins looks at me with a sombre expression, tinged with annoyance at what he knows I'm about to say.

"You've got that look, Alex."

"What look?"

"That look when you're about to tell me something you know I won't like."

He knows me too well.

"You two take the truck back to base. Get everyone ready. I need to find out what happened here."

"You can't be serious—you're going out there on your own?"

Sheppard butts in. "More importantly—you're takin' my ride?"

"I'll look after it, Shep."

She looks at both of us reluctantly before handing over the keys.

"You break it, you bought it," She pulls two large jerry cans and some water and rations from the rear of the truck, securing them in the back of the ATV. "This should get you to wherever you're going. Getting back may be a different story."

"If I don't find anything within a day, I'll head back. If anything goes wrong and you don't hear from me in 48 hours, move out and follow my trail. It's as good a place to start as any. We need to find somewhere relatively safe to settle."

Wilkins looks concerned, but he knows he can't talk me out of it.

"Be careful, my friend. It's a crazy post-apocalyptic world out there."

We embrace. "Still, it's home—or at least it used to be. Maybe it can be again," I say.

Sheppard laughs. "Ever the optimist. See you when you get back. "When" being the operative word."

I hug her quickly. "I'll do my best. Now get out of here. Only one passenger required in the Mystery Machine."

"Please don't call it that." Sheppard says with a furrowed brow. She's half serious.

I hop into the ATV and watch as the truck moves off, accelerating into the darkness. I take the driver's seat, and find that Sheppard has sneakily adjusted it to the most uncomfortable position imaginable. Nice move Shep.

After a few minutes fumbling with the seat settings, I start it up and slip into gear, switching on the front floodlight so I can follow the trail. I know I'm giving away my position, but it's the only way I can see. The desert resembles a lunar landscape in the dim moonlight, and probably has just as much life right now. The trail runs for several miles through a large canyon before sprawling into a sparse, flattened range, leading to a large rupture in the ground that once was a riverbed meandering into the distance. Looks like our mark is following this path.

Exhaustion is getting the better of me. I haven't slept in two days. I slug some of Sheppard's incredibly strong coffee from the flask she left behind. Hopefully it'll give me a little recharge. I need to decide whether to follow the river by the bank or just drive straight in. Whoever I'm following took the latter option, so I manoeuvre the ATV down the steep bank and begin the hunt.

After a few hours, I stop and exit to take a quick leak. There's a distinct change in the air. A breeze has blown up, but it's not the familiar desert breeze—it's more humid, you can almost smell the moisture in it. In the distance I can see clouds even blacker than the night rolling in, tumbling through the sky like heavy smoke being exhaled from the heavens. An ominous boom of thunder shakes the entire ground, followed by several flashes of lightning. I've always hated lightning. My old grandfather used to say it was just God welding to calm me down. This is pretty rare for this area, but nowadays anything goes where the weather is concerned. The one constant in nature is that weather does whatever the hell it wants, whenever it wants, but the devastation of the last few years has made it even more unpredictable, so I don't underestimate it. I jump back into the ATV, and resume the trail, as droplets of rain spit on my windshield. I push on, paying close attention to my surroundings. The drizzle turns quickly to downpour. My trail has vanished and the rain is falling so hard I can hardly see, but the floodlight tells me enough to know that there is water beginning to flow, and that it's rising fast. I need to get out of this river bed before it becomes a river again.

This is not good, I've travelled over two miles trying to find somewhere I can exit, but the banks are too high on either side. If I don't find something soon I'm in trouble. I know this thing is amphibious, but it wasn't designed for flowing water. I stop briefly to look outside, opening the back door to peer out. The water is almost two feet deep already, and it's only been twenty minutes. This thing will start to float soon if the water level gets any higher, which means I've got no control.

As I reach for the door to close it, a heavy rumble approaches, I can't quite make it out, but it doesn't sound good. Just as I shut the door it hits, and everything goes dark.

CHAPTER 13

I wake with a start, not noticing the pain at first, until I try to move, and my head explodes with eye-watering agony. I smashed it on something when the flood hit and judging by the pains in my limbs, I was tumbled around a bit afterwards. The ATV is face down in the newly formed river, the cabin almost filled with water. I was thrown between the seat and the mangled support bars, which probably saved me from drowning, but now I can't move. I have no idea how long I've been here. A stream of daylight beams through one of the tiny side windows, so it's been at least a few hours, maybe even days. I try to free myself, but I'm wedged in here so tight I can hardly breathe.

God I'm hungry. My mouth feels like sandpaper.

I see a ration pack floating a few feet away and try to reach it, but my arms and shoulders won't budge. How the hell am I going to get out of this?

That's when I hear it. Something's moving out there. My mind races through every possible scenario. What it comes down to is whether this is a rescue or capture, and rescue seems highly unlikely. Do I shout to tell them I'm here or shut up and hope they leave so I can starve to death in peace?

That question is answered when a metallic object slams against the back door of the vehicle. It's been badly damaged and won't be opening by traditional means. Whoever it is, they're trying their best to gain access, but it's not happening. The sound stops and there is complete silence for a minute, followed by a tiny spark igniting from the top corner of the door. The spark transforms to a brilliant glow and begins to move steadily in the outline of a rectangle, raining sparks that dance on the water with tiny hisses. As the rectangle is completed, the glow fades, and the entire panel is torn away, the sunlight blinding me as I await my fate.

As my eyes become accustomed to the light, a figure appears, leaning in to look. It's an android. I haven't seen any like this before, throughout this war there were no humanoid machines. It looks almost new, covered in white armour, it's head human-shaped in every way—even with simple facial features. Now I just need to wait and see if it's going to free me or kill me.

It stares at me in silence for at least a minute, then raises its arm and waves, speaking with a voice I thought I'd never hear again:

"Man, Sheppard's gonna be pissed."

PART FIVE
COUNTDOWN

CHAPTER 14

"Sarah?"

"Take it easy Alex, I'll explain later. Let's get you out of this tin can first."

"Don't call it that, you know she doesn't like it."

He really is going to have a tough time explaining this to Sheppard.

You climb down, your enhanced robotic hands gripping like intricate vices to whatever fixed point is available to grab onto, and slowly lower yourself to where Alex is awkwardly pinned.

Al peers over the edge.

"Do you need assistance, Sarah?"

"I got it, Al."

Alex looks confused.

"Who the hell is that?"

"Alex—meet Al, formerly known as—"

"The AI? Seriously? You named it?"

"Everybody needs a name."

You locate the wrought iron bar that's pinning Alex to the hull. If it had bent even an inch more it would have crushed him. You grasp the bar at the optimum point and bend it towards you, being careful not to use too much force.

"You might want to hold on to some—"

Before you can finish, Alex drops from his position, falling headfirst into the water filling the cockpit. You grab him by his belted waist and haul him back up as he gasps for air, the sensitive pressure sensors preventing you from crushing his fragile bones as you lift him upwards, spitting stagnant water from his mouth. He's weak, cold and starving, and has probably been lying here unconscious for more than a day, but his vitals are good and although his limbs are stiff from being pinned where he was, there are no signs of breakage.

"Let's get you out of here—then we can talk."

You climb to the exit, carrying him easily with one arm, handing him to Al who carefully lifts him outside, placing him on the ground as you climb out yourself. Mayberry approaches, introduces himself, and offers Alex a canteen, warning him not to drink too fast, and a protein bar that probably tastes as bad as it looks. He needs to rest, and it'll be dark soon. Mayberry has started a fire, while Al and Alice disappear to search for more firewood, letting him sleep for a few hours. They've both become accustomed to their new android shells pretty quickly, and on more than a few occasions since Al was transferred from your system, you've noticed them both making common human gestures in a cute, but slightly creepy way. You feel guilty—this seems a lot like prejudice.

You spend the time figuring out how to explain all this to Alex. As soon as he wakes, he wants answers, so you sit down facing the crackling fire, and tell him everything, at least everything you remember. Although he's listening intently, you can tell by his face that he expects you to blame him for what you've become, for lying to you, but you know he had no choice. When you finish your story, you gently put a hand on his shoulder.

"It's okay Alex. I know. You did the right thing. If it were me, I would have done the same."

"I'm tired of doing the right thing Sarah. Every time I do, it turns out to be the wrong thing."

"If you hadn't, we'd all be dead right now."

He opens his arms wide, gesturing to your surroundings.

"Look around, Sarah—we might as well be."

"No!" you shout. The noise level, much louder than you expected, startles both Alex and Mayberry. Yet another feature you haven't quite mastered yet.

"I didn't go through all this for nothing Alex. If there's even the slightest chance we can survive, we have to take it—at whatever cost. We could be all that's left."

"We are all that's left. This world is dead."

Mayberry takes over the conversation.

"Then we need to bring it back to life."

He circles the fire, carefully poking the embers with a long stick, sending tiny sparks dancing into the air. "Our priority right now is finding the rest of the survivors and getting them to the facility. Al here reckons the explosion at the tower may have triggered the release of nano clouds, designed to obliterate any living thing that crosses their path."

"Some of the information Doctor Bentley kept from me was briefly accessible in the final moments of the explosion before he and the network were destroyed," Al says, "But only in minute segments of broken data. I've tried to retrieve as much as I can, but there are two things I know for certain—the clouds will find and kill any remaining survivors,"

You lean forward, "And the second thing?"

"There has been some activity in the underground area of the tower. I don't know what, just that some type of equipment was activated."

"More drones?"

"I doubt it. Very few resources remain on site to build anything of significance, and whatever is left of the facility would be running on very limited reserve power at best."

"Bentley mentioned that I wasn't the only subject for the transfer experiments. What happened to the others?"

"The only information I have is that the remains were kept in storage."

"And I presume the storage area was underground."

"Yes."

Alex looks troubled.

"We need to get back. Now."

"He's right," Mayberry agrees.

"I told them to leave if I didn't make it back. They could be moving already."

You stand, wiping the red dust from your white body armour.

"In that case, we've already gotten a late start. Let's go."

You look around the group. The conversation for the past hour has been so intense you didn't even notice. "Hey, where's Alice?"

Mayberry smiles. "Well, you're not going to get there in a tiny scout vehicle. I sent her back for something a little more—appropriate."

He barely finishes the sentence as the bouncing bright beams of a vehicle's headlights dart across the dark landscape in the distance. A few minutes later as it draws near, Alex looks bemused as the familiar purr of an engine approaches. It's another ATV similar to Sheppard's, except slightly larger, and in much better shape. Mayberry gathers his things and heads not towards the newly arrived vehicle, but his own.

"You're just full of surprises, Doc. You're not coming?"

"No, Sarah. I don't think I'd be of any use to you. I need to make preparations for the new arrivals, providing you can get them back safe, of course."

"What kind of preparations?"

"For transfer. I need to start building new units."

"Whoa, Doc. You're saying you want them back here so you can turn them into—"

You gesture towards yourself.

"—cyborgs?"

Mayberry smiles. "I prefer the term "Remote Humans" but if you want to call them cyborgs, go right ahead. I just think it's a tad crude."

"Will they have a choice?"

"Absolutely. Life or death. The odds of survival are pretty slim if they remain as they are. Chances are, some are already sick or dying, and if they come in contact with the nano clouds then they're all dead. Transferring will buy them time, and can be reversed at a later stage if needed. It's the only long term chance of survival, and the fastest way to make it happen. Rebuild, then repopulate. There's no other way. Our priority right now is finding the rest of the survivors and getting them to the facility."

CHAPTER 15

The faint shimmer of the moon peeks curiously through the congested sky at random intervals. It's a rare sight these nights. Al and Alice retreat quietly to the shadows, probably the first chance they've had to spend time alone since they were reunited. She's quiet and soft spoken, almost timid, more than likely a result of Bentley's strange brand of relentless abuse over the years. You can't blame Al for keeping the fact that she still existed from you until the time was right. She's gotten used to her new form quickly, and seems genuinely relieved to be free. You start to wonder if this has changed your relationship with him. Now that he has Alice back, what will he do to protect her? Did he really do all this to help, or was his agenda all along purely to find her?

Mayberry wants someone to accompany him back to help with the preparations. After a brief discussion, Alice volunteers. She's been in the Facility's system long enough to know every single function and procedure down to the most minute detail, and is already figuring out ways to improve Mayberry's processes. In a moment that fascinates you, she and Al embrace, and he watches forlornly as she walks away from him. Two artificial beings drawn together by the most human of instincts.

Alex stands at your side, also watching with interest.

"This creeping you out, Alex?"

"No, quite the opposite. I find it strangely arousing."

You turn and lightly punch his shoulder, knocking him off balance. He staggers backwards slightly, but manages to retain his footing.

"Hey, careful with the Future Of The Human Race here, Robogirl."

He's joking, and it's funny, but part of you can't help thinking about how, unlike the survivors, you'll never have the luxury of being human again. You make a conscious decision not to dwell on it; you have to move on, make the best of it, do something with the chance you've been given. You probably would have died in that attack had Bentley not taken you. What good would you be then? You're right here, right now, and you can help in some way towards fixing what Bentley did. It'll take a hell of a long time before it makes any impact, but what else is there?

Al waves to Alice and Mayberry as the tiny electric vehicle is enveloped by the night, slipping away into the almost fluid darkness of the desert. You climb into the new and improved ATV and take a seat. Alex sits opposite. He still looks wary, and you can't blame him. It's a lot to take in, but time is running out for the others. There will be time to talk later.

Hopefully.

Al takes the wheel and the ATV jerks forward violently as it starts.

"Sorry," he says. "I've never done this before, it may take a few minutes to get accustomed."

Alex sniggers. "All that intelligence and technology and still can't drive stick."

Al turns to him. "So Alex, how did your last driving experience work out for you?"

"Harsh, man. Harsh."

"Okay you guys," you say. "If we come across any remaining walls on the way, you're more than welcome to continue your little pissing contest there."

"But I can't—oh. Sorry, Sarah."

"Just drive, Al."

Alex smiles, and for the first time since you were reunited, it actually feels like he's smiling at you, and not some machine that acts and thinks like you, and even though your new visage can only manage basic features, you smile back in the best way you can. He makes himself as comfortable as possible and tries to get some sleep, while you power down to active sleep mode to conserve energy. It's the closest thing you'll ever get to resting, and whatever algorithms the process utilises, it feels mildly pleasurable, giving you an almost weightless feeling while still being aware of your surroundings.

A few hours pass, and the dawn struggles to break through the morning sky. You reactivate and gently shake Alex to wake him. He jolts upward, forgetting where he is momentarily, drool dripping down his chin, and mucus-filled eyes gluing his eyelids shut. He's quite the sight. As he collects himself, you open the roof hatch to take a look outside. You've followed the riverbank back, a couple of hills to cross and what's left of the Tower should be visible soon. You scan the area, watching the crimson clouds tumble across the sky like blood through water, backlit by the rising sun.

It happens so quickly not even your enhanced body can react fast enough. A sharp metal clang is followed by several more in quick succession as a hail of bullets begins to strike the vehicle. Too late, you try to duck down as your haptic sensors detect an almighty collision from the high calibre bullet that strikes your head plate. The force knocks your head to one side, violently rocking your body as you struggle to hold on. You hear Alex yell your name as warning lights flash on your display. Emergency diagnostics activate and for a few brief seconds you are totally disorientated. Alex grabs you and drags you back inside as another slew of bullets narrowly misses you, spitting dust as they bury themselves deep in the ground. He screams at Al.

"Go!"

Al floors the pedal, engaging a booster to gain extra speed and find cover. The tough outer plating on the ATV, while protecting those inside, does so at a cost; the heavier vehicle isn't as fast as it could be, but there's a small canyon up ahead that should provide protection if you can reach it in time.

"Stay with me, Sarah."

Alex checks your head for damage, but the combination of high tech materials used in your construction seems to have done the job. Your systems calm down as the diagnostics reveal no major damage, just a cosmetic mark where the bullet struck.

"You're okay. Nothing a paint job can't fix. Looks like they might have sent someone looking for me. They were probably spooked by the different ATV."

"I don't think we need to worry about aesthetics right now, but if they're following your trail, they may come in contact with Mayberry and Alice, and that might not end well."

"Alice has been configured as a security grade unit," Al says. "She will be able to protect herself and Doctor Mayberry in the event of an attack."

"That's what I'm afraid of, Al."

While the impact didn't hurt as such, it was definitely a disturbing sensation. You pick yourself up and peer through the tiny apertures in the hull. A quick scan of the area outside reveals three heat signatures almost a half mile away, but that seems to be all. The others haven't made it this far yet, but they could be headed in this direction soon. There's no point in trying to communicate with them right now. It's possible that they have RPG's, and not even this boat will withstand an RPG strike. Best to move on, and try to establish contact using Alex.

You're out of range within a few minutes, and no one's following. They may have been able to alert others though, so you need to tread carefully. Al disengages the booster to conserve energy as the ATV rumbles through a cramped valley. Dawn eventually gives way to morning and soon after, the remains of the Tower come into view in the distance, still smouldering like a gigantic burnt match stuck into the ground. You cautiously open the roof hatch again, peering outside. Ordering Al to stop, you steady yourself enough to engage your telescopic sight, magnifying slowly to avoid disorientation. At two hundred times magnification you can make out the tracks of a vehicle, although the resolution is vastly reduced thanks to the digital zoom. They lead towards the base. Looks like someone got curious.

As you approach the base, you see the truck parked near the entrance hatch. Odd that it was left there, they should have driven it underground. In the distance a remote dozer creeps slowly across the landscape, like a sad old dinosaur searching for a lost companion.

The plan is for Alex to contact the base alone first, giving him time to explain the situation. Bringing you and Al with him isn't an option; these people have spent their entire lives running from machines, and although none of them may have looked like you, they're likely to be hostile, and you can't blame them for that. Instead, you'll wait out of sight, perched on the wall of what's left of a nearby building. You can see and hear everything from that vantage point, and intervene quickly if needed.

You exit the vehicle as Alex takes the driver's seat, and run to the crumbling building, quickly scaling the wall and positioning yourselves out of sight. Alex drives slowly and steadily towards the base, giving a verbal confirmation every minute to confirm the audio signal.

So far, so good.

He's coming close to the base entrance now.

You can see camouflage move as the hatch opens, and two figures climb out. It's Sheppard and Wilkins. Sheppard is unarmed, while Wilkins holds a pulse rifle, aimed squarely at the ATV as it nears them.

Audio is a little patchy, but should be good enough to pick up the conversation.

The ATV brakes, jumping forward suddenly as a distracted Alex forgets to disengage the gearbox, then comes to a sudden stop. Al can't help but smile, as do you.

"Nice comedy stop, Alex,"

Alex replies, but a sudden blast of interference drowns out most of it. From the parts you heard, that's probably a good thing.

The rear door opens as Alex disembarks, unarmed, with his hands raised. You zoom to his location in time to see him approach Sheppard with caution. She stands her ground defensively, her tall frame towering over her companion, and nods towards the ATV.

"What did you do, Alex? What did you do? Where's my ride?"

Alex edges forward, arms still raised.

"Relax, Shep. I traded it in for the new model."

"I liked the old model. More importantly, where did you get it?"

"We have a lot to discuss. Gather the others."

A tremor develops in her voice.

"I can't let you in, Sir,"

Wilkins raises his rifle, aiming directly at Alex. He looks shit scared. Alex has already begun lowering his arms, and quickly raises them again, shaking his hands to emphasise his compliance.

"Whoa. It's me, Shep. What's going on?"

"Where is she?"

"Where's who, Shep?"

Something isn't right.

"Where's Sarah?"

How could she know?

"Alex, you need to get out of there. Something's wrong."

This isn't going as planned. Alex scratches his head to signal that he understands and slowly backs away from Sheppard and Wilkins.

"Sarah's dead Shep. She died in the Tower. You know that."

Wilkins looks concerned and walks closer to Sheppard.

"You okay Shep? It's Alex, Sarah's gone," he says.

"No she isn't."

Without even looking at him, she grabs Wilkins by the throat, lifting him almost a foot off the ground. He drops the rifle and frantically grabs her arm trying to free himself, flailing wildly, but it's no use.

"Sheppard! What are you doing? Stand down, that's an order!"

"WHERE IS SHE?"

She turns to face Wilkins as he fights for breath, both hands grabbing her arm, desperately trying to free himself, his skin quickly changing colour, his pleading eyes bulging fiercely as he tries to kick free with his dangling legs, but she's not letting go.

You jump from the watchtower. It's a twenty foot drop and you land with a dusty thud, and sprint towards the base. Al follows suit. You're not going to reach them in time.

"Al, you get Alex. I'll handle Sheppard."

Al breaks from your side and heads in Alex's direction. You increase speed as Wilkins' body begins to go limp. Thirty seconds later, you're standing in front of them.

"Sheppard, please, stop. Let him go. I'm here. It's me."

She looks at you with a mixture of sadness and confusion, still not relaxing her grip on Wilkins. He doesn't have much time left.

"Sarah?"

She begins to cry.

"What's happening to me?"

"I'm not sure, please just let him go. We can work this out. It's me. I'm still me."

Her expression changes, and the crying face transforms to a smile. Except it's not a good smile, more of a sneer.

"You certainly are, Captain."

She twists Wilkins' neck. It makes an audible cracking noise as she discards him like a rag doll in the direction of the others, so quickly not even you have time to react. Alex screams in protest, but Sheppard takes little notice.

There's something in the way she uttered that last sentence.

It can't be.
No.

"Bingo!"

CHAPTER 16

You can't move. The sheer horror of hearing that word again brings it all back. Such a simple, whimsical word normally, and now it evokes so much pain and suffering.

Al stands beside Alex, who has dropped to his knees, unable to comprehend what's happening. As tough as you have all become over the years, sometimes there's no other possible reaction to something like this.

"Well, Sarah—"

"I swear to God, Bentley—if you say "We meet again," I will disassemble myself."

Bentley grins, but that trademark grin doesn't belong to him.

"Where's Sheppard?" you ask.

"Oh she's still here. I'm not quite finished with her yet."

"You know, I didn't want to say anything, but you really have a penchant for ladies' bodies. You sure there wasn't some other underlying reason for your psychosis?"

"Very funny. But you see—"

"Ah, whatever. Spare me the Scooby Doo episode Doc, I've already been through that, and I'm not sure I can stand another performance."

Bentley looks at Al.

"So she gave you a name."

Al looks at him timidly, the look of someone desperately trying to confront their abuser and not break down. It's the first time you've seen him like this since the Tower.

"Everybody needs a name."

"But you're a nobody. You're nothing. I created you to serve me, and you couldn't even get that right."

"Leave him alone."

"I knew you'd be trouble, but I guess I've only got myself to blame. Only one thing to do now I suppose."

"Really, and what's that?"

"Push the button."

As he utters the last word, he raises his arm to reveal a trigger mechanism.

Al and Alex have already started pulling Wilkins behind the ATV, and you scream at them to get down.

The ground beneath you rumbles intensely, followed quickly by a massive explosion, spewing a wall of earth and sand into the air, blowing you onto your back. The ground beneath Bentley opens and he falls through. He timed this to perfection, as the area where he falls leads to the escape tunnels. You look down in time to see him dart forward as the tunnel collapses behind him, and the entire base implodes in a maelstrom of whirling dirt.

Al and Alex were shielded by the ATV and are attending to Wilkins, although debris is still raining down, and visibility is non-existent. You can hear Alex shouting at Wilkins to stay with him, but you already know that he's not going to survive. You reach them and kneel beside Alex. Wilkins is fading fast, blood running from his nose and down the side of his mouth. He's trying to speak, but the blood is filling his mouth quicker than he can spit it out.

"What happened, Wilkins?"

"W-we went to the Tower...s-something, t-took Shep. I woke up and she was back, but d-different. I d-didn't know what she was going to do."

"What about the others?"

"Gone."

"She killed them?"

"N-no."

"Th-"

"They're"

"N.."

"Not."

"H-"

"Here."

He barely gets the last word out before he passes. Alex strokes Wilkins' forehead gently, gathers himself and stands, looking around at the blast area.

"They actually did what I told them for once. But where the hell did they go?"

"Not the way we came. The scouting party must have been going in the opposite direction. Looks like they're headed the wrong way. We need to find them before Bentley does."

You can't follow him through the tunnels, but it'll take Bentley a while to find his way out, so that'll buy you precious time. Alex takes the truck while you jump in the ATV with Al and negotiate your way around the huge crater where the base used to be. Eventually you find the tracks leading away from the base. They don't have much time left. Supplies were almost depleted after Davis and the others left, and only two small vehicles remained, with limited fuel, and it's likely the scouting party took one of them. Analysing the tracks, it looks like they've got a few hours headstart.

The radio buzzes in a burst of spitting static.

"Guys, we have another problem. Look east."

You stop the vehicle and open the roof hatch, scanning eastward. A dark cloud is forming in the distance, but something's not quite right. It's almost too dark, and swirls in a strange fashion unlike any cloud you've seen. As you try to check the wind speed, it reveals something even more horrifying.

It's moving toward you—against the wind.

"Shit. We need to get out of here. Fast."

Al resumes driving at increased speed, in spite of your dwindling fuel and energy. Even if you reach them now, will you have enough to get them back to the Facility? You're looking at over forty people and three vehicles. But you've got to catch up with them first, and outrun a nano cloud, not to mention a deranged genocidal maniac.

Al has no knowledge of the nano cloud's structure or purpose, and wasn't involved in its creation, so all you know is that if it reaches the survivors, it will most likely kill them on contact, and could also attack your systems and hardware.

Even with your increased processing power, you're struggling to find a way out of this, and for the first time since your encounter with the quadras, you begin to feel the stress of what you've been tasked with, or at least what you perceive as stress—now it's just algorithms based on your former brain patterns. With each passing hour, your mind gradually becomes more accustomed to its new home, but you fear that at some point you may cease to be human altogether. Could that happen? Will you continue to exist as Sarah, or will you just become an emotionless automaton? You've lost so much already. At least the others have a chance. It won't be a one-way trip for them. It may take some time, but eventually they'll be able to return to their human forms. Not so for you, Al or Alice. Of course they don't know any better—they've never been human, but there will come a point where you have to let go, and fully embrace what you've become.

No time to dwell on that now.

The radio crackles as Alex hails you again.

"You guys see that ahead?"

The terrain has flattened to an open plain, and just on the horizon, only a few miles away, the wheels of the remaining vehicle send a cloud into the darkening sky, a dusty beacon betraying the survivor's position.

They have no idea what's coming.

PART SIX
COLLISION

CHAPTER 17

"What the hell was that?"

Denton looks upward as the dust cloud from the explosion mushrooms into the morning sky, sucking up everything beneath it and spitting it violently into the atmosphere.

"Jesus, that's the base. Was it rigged to do that when they left?" Blunt says.

"Not that I know of. Why would they go to that effort?"

Denton leans forward, cupping his hand to direct his voice toward the driver.

"We need to move faster, Walters," he orders. "That transport we fired on must have reached the base already."

"Who do you think it was?" asks Walters, shouting over the incessant whine of the ailing engine.

"No idea, but considering we're all that's left, my guess is some sort of raiding party to finish us off."

"Maybe it was Alex."

"That wasn't Sheppard's ATV, so we don't know what we're dealing with,"

"Other survivors?"

"I doubt it. Sheppard said Alex headed south," Denton says. "Either way, we need to catch up with the others fast."

The three don their dust masks once again as Walters guides the three-seated vehicle, aptly named The Ferret, in the direction of the explosion, gaining speed, the relentless barrage of sand and dust against the cracked and stained windscreen making visibility almost impossible.

The vehicle hits a large mound, catapulting itself into the air and landing roughly, the large suspension throwing the passengers around the inside of the vehicle like rag dolls. Denton grabs a guardrail to steady himself as the vehicle regains traction and continues through the rough terrain.

A few minutes later, the landscape plateaus onto the sparse plain, with the Tower clearly in sight to the west. Walters veers right and heads east in the direction of the base. Denton stares at the Tower as they pass. What remains is now crumbling to the ground.

A lone figure comes into view in the distance, walking slowly, its shape distorted by the rising heat on the horizon, making it difficult to discern who it could be. When it's a few hundred yards away, Walters hits the brakes and all three alight, raising their weapons to eye level. Denton squints, trying to focus on the approaching person, and before he can shout at the figure to raise its hands, both shoot into the air, waving wildly. As the figure comes closer, Denton breathes a sigh of relief as he recognises who it is.

"Sheppard?" he shouts.

Sheppard runs towards them. She looks dishevelled, her hair is matted with blood and her fatigues are torn and blackened, but she doesn't seem to be badly hurt.

She nods upwardly, partly a greeting, partly a lazy salute.

"Dent."

"Shep. What happened? Where the hell did you come from?"

"Wilkins and I just got back to the base and there was an explosion. He's dead. The others had already left. They're about to meet a whole new breed of trouble. There are new robots. Humanoid ones, and they're heading straight for them. Oh, and there's that."

She points to the area between the Tower and the base, where the nano cloud is moving.

Denton has a panicked look on his face as he addresses the others. "We need to get to them. Let's go."

Sheppard raises a hand.

"Not so fast, guys," she says, gesturing to the vehicle.

"I'll be needing this."

CHAPTER 18

As you near the convoy of survivors, you try to calculate how this is going to play out, but all the enhanced brain power in the world isn't going to come up with a solution to this. Even if you convince them to come with you, there's Bentley to contend with, not to mention this damn cloud.

The cloud seems to have stopped for now, and despite the wind it holds itself in position, swirling like a thick, weightless liquid through the air. Waiting, watching.

Alex is driving parallel to you, edging forward with a mixture of determination and desperation, knowing what has to be done, but having no clue how to achieve it. He's the key here; they won't listen to you. He needs to persuade them to come with you.

Provided any of you survive, that is.

Still no sign of Bentley. Where the hell is he?

Part of you can't help wondering what drove him to this. Was it just sheer psychosis, a by-product of the transfer, or was it his plan all along? From what you gleaned from Mayberry, he had a pretty normal life up to that point, and you could certainly see how transferring could drive a certain mind to madness, but Bentley was highly intelligent, much more than you. He must have been able to cope. You worry about the others. Will they be able to handle it? Could some be too scared to undergo the process? Could some be driven mad like Bentley and be a danger to the others? It doesn't matter; there's no other way. They can't survive as they are. At least this way there's some chance, and you owe it to them to take it. They're not just survivors—they're your friends, your family, your people. Everything you've done up to this point was to keep them safe, and whether they like it or not, you're going to do just that.

The radio crackles again.

"Pull back, I'm going to go talk to them. I'll contact you as soon as it's safe to approach. I'm sending Al over to you."

"I really don't think my safety is an issue here, Alex."

"True, but I don't want them wasting valuable ammo on you."

"Always a pal. Fair enough."

Without the truck even slowing, Al bounds from the rear, hits the ground running, and veers toward you. You slow to a stop and he waits outside. You get out and join him.

"Now what, Al?"

"Whatever happens, unless we find Doctor Bentley—"

"Stop calling him that."

"What?"

"Doctor. Doctors help people, even the academic ones."

"Very well. Unless we find Bentley, we're never going to be safe."

You sigh, purely a sound effect now, but necessary.

"Somehow I don't think that's going to be too hard."

The plain is so flat now, you can see for miles into the distance. Zooming as far as your lenses will allow, you can just about make out the dust cloud of another approaching vehicle.

You both wait. A familiar pang of anxiety simmers briefly in your consciousness, although it feels different now, more manageable, a simple blip to be purged from your stream of thought by whatever programming trickery is controlling your very being. It's hard to describe, but it gives you an advantage. All those chemicals that once raced through your body, sometimes causing happiness, sometimes love, sometimes chaos—they are no more. You can't help but wonder if it will eventually make you colder, more calculating.

Less human.

You see Alex approaching the camp in the truck. A crowd gathers around him, some with weapons raised, but they quickly drop and some run to embrace him. He beckons the entire crowd to assemble, and they begin to form a circle around him, engulfing him until he's out of sight.

"Damn it Alex, why you have to be such a short-ass?"

Ten minutes later, the radio spews a burst of static followed by his voice.

"Okay, I think they're ready to see you."

Al is already waiting at the wheel of the ATV. You hop on board and grab a guard rail with one had to steady yourself as he accelerates forward, the ATV's ageing gears grinding in protest initially, then finally slipping into place as it cruises toward the camp.

As you draw closer, the crowd split from the circle, opening out to a straight line. There are fifty, maybe sixty people left at most. Alex steps forward, ever the leader, as your vehicle comes to a halt twenty feet away. You open the door and jump out, your heavy frame kicking fine dust into the air as your feet hit the ground. Al is still at the wheel.

"Wait here, Al."

He nods, remaining alert.

You begin to walk. The wind has died down temporarily and the uneasy quiet is broken only by the sound of your servos pushing you forward; a soft, whirring mechanical sound, followed by a metallic clunk each time your feet move forward. For a second, you almost forget yourself, stumbling slightly until your gyros kick in and correct your balance.

You stand facing Alex, unsure of what to do next. Each person gazes at you with the blank stares of those with nothing left to lose. Dishevelled and broken, hungry and afraid, they've all been through so much. Alex steps aside and you walk forward to face them.

"This," Alex says, gesturing to you, "Is Sarah Ford. Your captain. She's been through a lot, more than you could imagine. And she did it all for you—each and every one of you. She's given up her flesh and blood, but not her humanity. She's still the same Sarah we've all known. The fighter, the leader, the friend, the comrade. Unfortunately she also still has the same sense of humour, and god awful taste in music, but you can't win 'em all."

His quip draws a few smiles. Even now, in this barren, dead place, in this seemingly impossible situation, someone can smile.

Then it hits you. A flood of memories released in one sharp burst, everything that's happened, from the fifteen year-old girl without a care in the world, to what stands before them now. For the first time since the initial transfer, a barrage of emotions assault you, overwhelming even the sophisticated programming that simulates your former humanity. You drop to your knees, head in hands, unable to cry, save for one single sob.

You remain on the ground for what seems like an age, until a loud cracking noise breaks the silence, followed quickly in succession by another. A second, then a third, then a fourth join in, with more following suit. Are they—

Clapping?

The claps accumulate until everyone joins in, a rapturous, enthusiastic applause. Alex stands at your side, joining in, smiling, his eyes becoming glassy as tears begin to well up. The crowd once again circles around you and Alex. Brady breaks from the group and faces you, extending her hand to reaffirm the friendship you once knew. The shake quickly transforms to an embrace, and although it probably feels odd for her, hugging a hunk of metal and plastic, your haptic sensors do the best job they can of making it feel wonderful.

"We missed you, Captain," she says, her pale sickly demeanour for a brief moment replaced by a faint reddish glow.

There's no time for this.

You look at Alex. "Did you explain the situation?"

"Yes, it's unanimous. Everyone is in."

"It's not like we really have any choice," Brady adds. "I just have one demand."

"What is it?" you ask.

"Can my new body have a smaller butt?"

"I'll see what I can do," you laugh.

The brevity is shortlived as a shout comes from behind you.

"Something's coming!"

You pivot around on one foot, zooming in on the approaching vehicle.

"It's the scouting party," says a man holding an oversized scope. The blazing sun has poked a searing hole through the clouds to the west, and coupled with the diffusing haze of dust and sand makes it almost impossible to focus on the incoming arrival. Minutes later, it comes more plainly into view. You are unable to see the driver, but something else gets your attention. Something behind the scout vehicle is kicking up dust also. Is there something following it? You zoom again and refocus, the light still affecting your optics, making them recalibrate to the insanely busy panorama before it, compensating for glare, filtering out the brightness and contrasting the dark until you can finally see what the others can't.

No.

The shapes behind the scout vehicle aren't following it—they're being dragged behind it. A scan of the cockpit confirms only one occupant. The Ferret approaches at speed, and veers to one side before it stops, causing what's being dragged behind it to swing around in a wide arc before eventually skidding to a stop in front of it, just a few hundred feet from where you're standing.

A detail disperses from the crowd, rifles raised, targeting Bentley as he brazenly steps out in Sheppard's body, almost strutting, opening out his arms to display his handiwork. The mangled bodies of the scouting team are unrecognisable, torn to shreds over sharp rock on the journey here. You can't even imagine what they went through.

To the right, someone shouts "It's Sheppard, hold your fire!"

"No," Alex shouts. "It's Bentley. Stay in formation and keep her in your sights!"

Al comes to your side. Bentley is just standing there defiantly.

"What's he doing?" Alex asks.

"At least he's not talking, but I doubt he's here for a chinwag at this point in our relationship."

Minutes pass, no one moves. Bentley seems frozen to the spot.

"Sarah, remember what happened on the way here?"

"Oh shit," you gasp, just as you see Bentley break from his frozen stance and reach into the cockpit to retrieve Denton's RPG, raising it to eye level as he swings around to face you.

There's little time to react. The armed ones open fire, a volley of bullets spit through the desert air, almost leaving a trail behind them as they zip through the dust, slamming into Bentley as he prepares to fire. The bullets seem to have little effect other than tearing tiny holes in Sheppard's flesh, revealing the shining metal underneath. Part of you knows there's no hope for Sheppard, and while it saddens you deeply, there's no time to mourn her now.

"Get down!" you scream to the others as they disperse in wild panic, completely confused and terrified.

The first rocket hits the truck, the extra fuel being carried amplifying the explosion as a deadly blast of air and metal sprays from it. Several pieces of shrapnel slam against you, one skimming against your head, but your motorised reflexes throw you to the ground in a split second.

"She's reloading!" comes a cry from your left. It's Alex. He's been hit, part of his upper arm sporting a large chunk of metal. You jump to your feet as quickly as you dropped. Too late. Bentley has already loaded another rocket, and this one is pointed straight at the crowd.

A connection signal bleats as a burst of information hits you faster than you can even process. It's Al communicating with you purely by data, just like before, back at the Tower. You understand the instruction and instantly act, grabbing a large piece of metal debris and signalling Al, who is standing twenty feet away doing the same. There's only one chance for this to work, the calculations have been done and just seconds to act. You both work in tandem, almost as if you are one. You know this isn't the right time, but it feels oddly pleasurable.

Not now, Ford.

The others look on helplessly as Bentley pulls the trigger, the force of the rocket exiting the weapon pushing him backward. Time slows, almost to a standstill, as the rocket launches, leaving a thick trail of smoke in its wake as it snakes through the air, heading straight for the group, now huddled together in fear. A subroutine kicks in, doing the work for you as your arm servos are boosted and you both hurl the pieces of metal at the rocket, the trajectory of each perfectly programmed to hit the rocket at that exact point in space. Immediately after throwing your projectiles, you both drop to the ground, as they both hit at precisely the same time and the rocket explodes in mid-air. While it is still quite close, the impact is far less devastating than it could have been.

Bentley calmly drops the weapon to the ground, as if he were a bored infant discarding a toy, and jumps back onboard the Ferret, speeding away, not even having the decency to cut the scouting party's bodies loose, and three sickening trails of dark red follow him into the distance. Several people fire on the vehicle as it leaves, but the ammunition is wasted. You yell at them to stop, but they already know they're wasting their time, it's just a rage-filled response now.

The truck has been obliterated, months of supplies gone in an instant. You look around the camp as the others begin to take stock after the attack. They look so weary and terrified, they're not even soldiers anymore. There have been several fatalities, two who were standing by the truck when it was hit, and one who stood beside you, taking the worst of the shrapnel that missed you.

Brady.

You fall to your knees beside her, as the last gasp of air escapes her lungs, her eyes still, a large piece of metal lodged in her throat, the entire front of her uniform stained with congealing blood. From the back of the crowd, someone rushes forward, keening uncontrollably as she too falls to her knees, looking to you with pleading eyes as if there's something you could do.

"I'm sorry, Grace." you say as sympathetically as your speech synthesis will allow. "She's gone."

Relationships were not encouraged during the war, but sometimes there are things you just can't control, and the attraction between them was insurmountable from the moment they met. That they should be parted now, so close to having a chance at a better life, just isn't fair after everything you've all been through.

She hugs her lost love, ignoring the blood, not caring that it is smearing on her face and clothes, not moving for several minutes, until Alex gently pats her shoulder.

"Grace—I'm so sorry, but we have to leave now, or every one of us is going to die."

She nods quietly, blood, mucus and tears coalescing with the dirt and dust on her face, and kisses Brady on the forehead, brushing away a stray strand of hair covering her eye as if it still needed to be done, and whispers softly in her ear as if persuading a child to sleep, laying her gently on the ground.

"Night, Sweets. I'll see you soon."

She rises to her feet, wiping her face with her sleeve, and turns to face you.

"Tell me you're going to kill him."

You put a hand on her shoulder.

"With gusto."

CHAPTER 19

Alex and Hoffman have started to round the others up, issuing the order to move out. There is little time to deal with the dead—now five in total, so a quick and shallow mass grave is all you can manage. The group look on, pausing briefly as the last shovel of dirt is heaped on the final resting place of your friends. Grace pulls a chain she wears from around her neck, not bothering to open it. It snaps easily and she looks at it tearfully for a moment, before hanging it from a makeshift cross fashioned from some splinters of wood left over from crates in the exploded truck. It's not really a cross—religion hasn't been a thing here for many years, no one who has seen what you've seen could possibly still believe that anyone cared for the human race now, but more a symbol of a loving memory.

As she walks away, she turns to you again.

"Will I still remember her, after all this is done?"

"Yes. You could choose not to, you know. If this works, you'll be around for quite some time to come, maybe too long to carry all that grief."

"No, it's my memory, it's my grief. It's all I have left now."

She's right of course, but you felt obliged to give her the choice. Which introduces another issue with these people transferring. Many have suffered so much already. Mayberry's taking a big gamble on them being stable enough to cope with the process, not to mention the work ahead of them.

"Hey, we want you to rebuild the human race—no pressure."

As everyone gathers what's left of their belongings and prepares to move out, you spot a large crow swooping down, perching itself on the cross. It bellows a hoarse cawing sound, as if in anger, perhaps a warning. There are few species of animal left, but it's not surprising that those flying rats managed to make it.

You pick up a stone, and fling it in the carrion eater's direction, deliberately missing it, but sending a clear message as it flies away, still cawing in defiance.

"Go harbinge somewhere else, asshole."

You were never one for metaphors.

There's only one route to get to the Facility on time, and it means following Bentley's trail. Seems you originally took a slightly longer route, so Al has recalculated for the optimum journey time. Alex jokingly calls it the Yellow Brick Road, Al doesn't get the reference. At some point it's inevitable that you'll be seeing Bentley again, and you hope Mayberry has protocols in place if he discovers it. Al scans through the schematics for the project that created your hybrid body, trying to find a weakness other than a sneakily-planted explosive. It's likely the process of transforming Sheppard was rushed and incomplete, but you can't take any chances.

Supplies are almost depleted. The remaining water might last most of the journey if rationed, but you'll be lucky if food lasts another day. You've got to get them to the facility as quickly as possible, and there's no choice but to go on foot.

The crowd waits, ready to move out on Alex's order, they already look exhausted. Their clothes are filthy and ragged, what little they have packed into makeshift rucksacks. They look more like a bunch of vagrants than the saviours of the human race, but they'll have to do. The weaker and injured members have been crammed into the ATV with Alex at the wheel, while you and Al lead on foot. Grace joins you, sporting the remaining pulse rifle. She's a crack shot, so it's in good hands. A few minutes later, Hoffman sidles up beside you, shines a snaggletoothed grin, and manages a shoddy salute. "Good to have you back, Captain."

Only a handful of weapons remain—several handguns and shotguns, some automatic rifles, Grace's pulse rifle and a couple of grenades, with hardly enough ammo to weather any kind of attack. Again, they'll have to do.

All this time, the nano cloud just loiters in the distance, swirling around like an enormous festering mass. It hasn't followed Bentley, nor does it seem to have acknowledged you and the survivors.

The ATV slowly accelerates, leaving a trail of parallel lines in the sand as the convoy moves out, fifty four tired souls going either to their redemption, or their doom, depending on how all this pans out. You communicate privately to Al.

"So, what do you think our chances are?"

"Statistically? Forty per cent."

At least he didn't say "We're doomed!"

"However, I've come to a conclusion about statistics. If there's one trait I admire in humanity, it's your ability to constantly—"

"Survive?" you interject.

"No, surprise."

The first few miles take you back past the Tower, this time going further west, not following the river as before. The smouldering has reduced to faint wisps, quickly dissipated by the hot winds. This is the closest anyone besides you has been to it and lived to tell the tale. Some look at it in amazement as you pass, some with disgust, some don't look at all, just keep their heads down and continue walking.

After almost twenty uneventful miles, huge concrete pillars appear on the horizon, defiantly jutting out of the sand, like buried fingers clawing their way out from underground. As you near them, you see they're the stanchions of an old off-ramp, the road sections long destroyed. This could mean there's a road nearby, or at least the remains of one. You'll need to camp for a few hours to allow the others to rest. What little food is left is rationed out, while Grace and Hoffman leave to try and hunt for food. There isn't much left to hunt in these parts any more, but certain small animals have miraculously survived and have been found thriving in some areas. The others make themselves as comfortable as they can, some sleeping rough on the ground, some in tattered tents, others don't sleep at all.

You and Al scout the area on foot, you need to save fuel in the ATV, and even as it is, it most likely won't make the full journey unless you get lucky with some extra sunlight, or Mayberry can arrange a fuel dropoff. You follow the pattern of the ruined off-ramp for a few miles, which does eventually lead to the remains of an old road, partly covered in sand now, but its shape is still faintly visible, at least enough to follow. If old maps are anything to go by, this road follows a similar path as the riverbed, save for a brief detour which looks like it may have once been a large town or city. There's no information available for the area, and no one from the group has been that far in this direction before, so you'll just have to wait and see.

You return to the camp and report to Alex. Hoffman and Grace have returned empty-handed, both looking disappointed but not surprised. What's left is rationed out as fairly as possible, keeping enough for another day at most. Water supplies are still holding, and after a few hours rest, spirits have improved somewhat.

It's the middle of the night as you resume your journey. It's best to stop when there's light to allow for any necessary recharging. The ATV's lights guide the way until you reach the road. After several miles, the road begins to show in places, with patches of the cracked grey asphalt appearing like sores in the beige sand. You and Al flank each side of the caravan, keeping a close eye out for any threat. Your night vision makes everyone radiate with an eerie green glow, as if they were ghosts trudging through the barren landscape. Every now and then, the faint outline of a small dog-like animal appears, following you at a safe distance, keeping pace. It is soon joined by several others, curious about this strange procession slowly making its way through their territory. They don't look big enough to be dangerous, but best to keep an eye on them for now. The terrain, which up until now has been relatively flat, begins to rise, the incline increasing steadily until it becomes quite steep. Mountainous terrain scrolls slowly by, the incline requiring more effort from those on foot. They're tired enough already, and this won't help. There is some commotion at the rear of the group, quickly followed by a scream. Al runs to investigate, coming back seconds later, carrying a man who has collapsed. It's Ramirez. He was hit by shrapnel in the explosion, and infection has set in. Al runs to join the ATV, so he can try to squeeze him onboard. It's unlikely he'll survive the trip, but you have to give him a chance.

An hour later, he's dead.

You hit over thirty miles as dawn prepares to rise. This is the first break in the thick cloud that you've seen in quite some time. Maybe there's been another shift in the global weather pattern. These days, they can be sudden, and often severe, as you've already learned on the riverbank. For now though, you'll take it as a piece of old fashioned good luck. The road has improved at this point, probably untouched since the early attacks.

Up ahead, at the peak of the steep hill, the ATV comes to a halt, the brake lights glowing red with the ferocity of an awakened demon. Alex jumps out, the pre-dawn haze silhouetting him against the open, cloudless sky, and beckons to you. You jog toward him, signalling for Al to join you. As you reach the ATV, a tiny sliver of sun peeks over the horizon, spilling an orange glow across the land below. On the other side, the road runs downhill for over two miles into a deep valley, eventually leading into the remains of a town, long forgotten on any existing map. Some smaller buildings still stand intact, flanked by the skeletal remains of the larger ones. It looks more like a small town than a city on closer inspection, but it'll do for shelter from the sun for a few hours while you recharge the ATV. It seems to have escaped the devastation many other places suffered. There are no signs of major explosions, most of the buildings were already low level, most only two or three storeys high, probably due to the area being prone to earthquakes.

As you begin the descent, you turn to see everyone staring in the opposite direction. Even in the dim morning light, they can see the nano cloud has followed, still keeping its distance, but no less terrifying. What the hell is it doing? If Bentley wanted you dead, surely the cloud would have done its work by now. Unless of course, Bentley has no real control over it.

The sun rises majestically, as if to reassure those below it that everything is continuing as normal. You're reminded of an old TV show from your childhood. You can barely remember it now, but it featured a sun rising every morning with a child's face and a cute, infantile giggle. Somehow, the smell of that moment comes back to you. A sunlit kitchen, the TV prattling in the corner. The faint aroma of your mother's perfume mingles with the sweet smell of sugary breakfast cereal, the toaster busily browning fresh white bread, bacon and eggs sizzling together in perfect harmony in a crowded frying pan. Oh my God, those smells, those beautiful, heavenly aromas. You don't smell them of course, and you never will again. It's just the memory of it, but it feels so good, so vivid.

"Sarah?"

You snap out of your reverie, aware that time has passed. It all feels so far away now, a lifetime away. Al waits by a mangled road sign up ahead that once welcomed visitors to this place, pointing at it with both thumbs up. The only words visible on what's left are "er".

"Al, quit being a tourist."

You both scout ahead, entering the town through the main thoroughfare. It's a long street, quite wide, flanked on each side by the blackened stumps of palm trees. The streets are littered with abandoned vehicles, most burnt out, some crashed into walls or lamp posts, rusted beyond recognition. The windows of most buildings are gone, shattered by whatever hit this place. Some are boarded up, others just left to rot. The tattered fabric of store awnings flaps in the light breeze, bleached colourless from years of sun.

Something's not right.

Where are the bodies?

There should be something, skeletal remains, traces of clothing, but there's nothing. Several thousand people lived here and should have died here, but there's no sign of them. It's a ghost town with no ghosts. You think back to the old western movies your grandfather used to watch over and over again. They always had a place like this, where a lone horseman would slowly trot into town, streets deserted, curtained windows concealing townsfolk attempting to peek discreetly at the new arrival, who normally brought either doom or redemption with him, depending on what movie you watched.

This time the windows are empty, and there's no big showdown to be had. At least you hope so.

First things first; you need to find shelter for the others. Halfway down the long street, a crossroads intersects. To the left, a large concrete building, still reasonably intact, save for a few broken windows, comes into view. It looks like a school, and one that had been built not long before the attacks, judging by the condition and difference in style to the other local buildings. You and Al walk up the short flight of steps to the entrance, unravelling the tangled chains holding the doors shut, and opening them. Fifteen years of stale air rushes forward as you step inside. A long corridor runs to the rear of the building, the only light coming through is from the tiny windows on the rows of classroom doors on each side, sending dusty beams across the otherwise darkened hallway. At the end, another pair of large double doors, also chained. There's something odd about the chains on the door. You walk forward, your optical filters compensating for the low light. As you near the doors, a large sign overhead reads "Auditorium". Each door has a small rectangular window just above the handles, but unlike the hallway doors, there is no light coming from these. At first glance it seems like they are covered with some sort of material, but as you draw closer and scan in more detail, the true horror of what you are seeing hits home. The material covering the windows is clothing, greyed over time. In the corner of one window, you see the ivory fingers of a skeletal hand. The chains weren't on the doors to keep people out—they were there to keep people in. The whole town must be in here, the pile of bodies at the door were those trying to escape, trampling each other in terror. Corralled and murdered like animals. You turn to Al.

"Did you know about this?"

"No Sarah, it looks like this happened during the first attacks, before I was activated. I'm not saying I'm not responsible for many deaths, just not these."

"The others can't see this," you say, and you both leave the school, replacing the chains on the entrance door. You both agree to come back before you leave, and burn it to the ground.

Alex joins you, having left the ATV at the edge of town with the others as they await the all clear. You tell him what you found at the school and dismiss it as a possible refuge for the night, agreeing to tell the others that there's serious structural damage. The three of you continue down the long street, until Alex stops in his tracks.

"You've got to be shitting me."

A few hundred yards down the street, a large banner is strung across the road, with tattered bunting and large hand-painted lettering festooned across.

W - E - L - C - O - M

A lone figure stands at the other end of the street, slowly ambling towards you. First reaction is that it's Bentley, but a quick scan reveals that it isn't. It's a man.

Alex raises his rifle, not taking any chances as the figure draws closer. He's a stocky fellow, dressed in a badly fitting black suit, a stained white shirt and a tie with a piano keyboard design on it, formerly white sneakers and a baseball cap adorned with a wolf emblem. A large ornate golden chain hangs from his shoulders, jangling as he walks forward with welcoming arms outstretched. Although he sees only Alex initially, as soon as he spots you and Al, he freezes and begins to turn on his heel.

"Wait," Alex hollers, loudly enough for him to be startled, lowering his rifle and holding out his arms. "We're not going to hurt you. We just need shelter."

He looks at Alex with suspicion.

"There are more of you? More like them," he says pointing to you and Al, "Or like you?"

Alex smiles that smile that leaves so many charmed and disarmed. "Nope, all human. They're just two of a kind, but we mean to make more. What's your name, friend?"

As he finishes the sentence, the ATV rolls into town, followed by the others.

"Well well, looks like I've got me some company," he says, raising a hand to the peak of his cap and lifting it off and back down again, briefly revealing a balding pate covered with a wisp of cow's lick. "Sorry about the banner—I didn't have time to finish it before you arrived, but you get the gist. Ned Travers, Mayor Ned Travers. Welcome to my town— or at least it was before all this kerfuffle."

Kerfuffle. Not exactly the best description for the End Of The World.

"Sure is nice to see a friendly face, though. It's been a long, long time since I had any company. You folks look like you could use a rest. Where ya headed?"

"South," Alex says, "Got some friends down there we need to find. You here all alone?"

Travers gazes wistfully at his laceless tennis shoes, and it's hard to read whether he's sad or ashamed. It's hard to imagine how anyone could have survived here for this long, and despite his odd-yet-harmless appearance, there's something not quite right with the Mayor.

"Yes, I've been alone here since the first attack. My daddy was what they used to call a prepper, one of those survivalist types. Had his own bunker and everything, all decked out with the best equipment, supplies and whatnot. People used to make fun of him, especially when he built the bunker. To be honest, I always thought he was a little crazy myself," He snorts a little, not quite a laugh, "But I'll be damned if he wasn't right all along. The day of the attack, all these drones appeared out of nowhere, just buzzin' around like huge insects. People were shit scared. Then this...thing—robot I suppose you'd call it appeared. We all thought it was a man at first because it was wearin' clothes—a long black coat with a sweatshirt, the hood up so we couldn't see his face properly; well, if you can call it a face. Said he was military issue, here to help, and told everyone to gather in the school auditorium for safety. They pretty much herded everyone in there."

Alex regards him as well as he can without seeming suspicious.

"And what about you?"

"Well, Dad wasn't believing any of it, and he knew this wasn't going to end well, so he told me he loved me (he'd never done that before, so I knew he was serious) and said to run home and get in the bunker. I said I didn't want to leave him, but I knew by the look on his face that he had already made up his mind what to do, so I told him the same, turned, and ran as he went to the truck and pulled out his M16 from behind the driver's seat and ran into the middle of the crowd, shooting at the drones. I could hear him screaming as I ran, cursing at those things zippin' around the sky. It was enough to distract them while I got away, but as I left, I could hear those things starting to fire on the people. Most were already inside the school at that point. All hell broke loose. I kept low and ran the mile or so back to our house. Man I thought my heart was going to explode in my chest, I don't think I've ever run so fast, or been so scared. So I got there, jumped in, and closed the hatch. Dad built it well, deep enough and shielded, so the drones' thermal scanners couldn't get through it. I just sat there and cried. I was fifteen years old."

His eyes well slightly and his lower lip quivers. It takes a lot of effort to keep his composure, but he keeps it together. This is probably the first time he's had to tell anyone what happened.

"I stayed down there for over a month. I hardly slept. I was waiting for the hatch to be torn open at any time, to be dragged out and killed, but it didn't happen. Dad had rigged up a sort of periscope so I could get a view of outside. For the first few weeks, the sky was full of those things, just hovering there like huge insects, but everyone was gone. Then one day, they just left. I was still too scared to go outside, but after a few more days I had to do something. I was getting a little stir crazy, hearing things, talking to myself. So I put on a gas mask (I had seen some weird coloured smoke around the centre of town), opened the hatch and went outside. It was so odd. There was no sound, no wind, no animals, not a bird in the sky. The silence was, well—deathly. I made my way back into town. The place looked pretty much as it does now—all shot up, trees burnt to a crisp, most of the windows broken. The larger buildings were levelled, like some big Godzilla monster had trampled on 'em. There was still no sign of anyone, just empty vehicles. I got to the school and saw the chain on the door. I didn't want to go inside, I knew what I'd find, but eventually, curiosity got the better of me. I knew they were all dead, my dad included, but man, when I saw those bodies piled in the auditorium, I lost my shit, ran outside, chained the door back up and ran back to the bunker as fast as I could. I never want to go back there. Think I must've puked three times on the way back, and some more after. Had to take off my mask, so good thing there wasn't anything bad left in the air."

He's visibly upset, and his story seems to check out.

"The real Mayor was one of the first to run to the school when the drones arrived. That coward didn't deserve the title, so I took it from him. He left this chain in his office, so I wear it every day since, in memory of the town. As long as I'm here, this town is still alive, even if I'm just Mayor of myself. I spent the next while stocking up on what supplies I could find. I've had enough to keep going until now, but I'm not sure how much longer they'll last."

Alex relaxes the grip on his rifle, acknowledging that the new arrival isn't a threat.

"So, Ned—I'm Alex, these are my friends Sarah and Al. We've got some sick, tired and hungry people here. Can you help us out? We'd be willing to take you with us."

Ned looks confused, if not a little conflicted. "I have some food and water, and the pharmacy is pretty much untouched, so you can grab whatever you can from there. I-I'm not so sure about leaving the town, though. I've been here all my life. Figured I'd die here. I owe it to them to stay," he says, beckoning to the school.

You move toward him. "Ned, those people are gone. Your father's gone. They need to be put to rest. Properly. You don't owe this town anything. There was nothing you could have done to help them. But know this—the thing you saw that day was once a man, and he's responsible for all this,"

Ned looks at you with welling eyes. "One man did all this?"

"Yes. He had some help, but he planned it, and he executed it. What he did here, he enjoyed. He did it for entertainment. And he's still out there. It's not safe for you here anymore."

"Look around, Mister—is it safe anywhere?"

"Fair point, but where we're going there's at least a chance."

Ned looks around, breathing in deeply, inhaling the air as if it were filled with the souls of the lost, and at that point, finally listening to what they tried to tell him all these years.

Let go.

"Can you promise me something, if you find him?"

"Yes, the same promise I've given everyone else."

Ned's demeanour brightens, his wide smile revealing several missing teeth.

"Well in that case I may have something of interest to you!"

Ned leads you and the group to shelter in an old church a few blocks down the street. One of the oldest structures there it has survived pretty much unscathed, save for a few broken windows. The pews serve as beds, not the most comfortable, but a damn sight better than the cold ground. Ned disappears, arriving back several minutes later with a shopping cart full of dried food, cans and bottled water. As everyone knows, this can be a lottery. For every can you open, some will be spoiled, some water will be stagnant, but anyone who has lived like this for any length of time will know the signs (and smells).

Thankfully, most of what Ned has brought is pretty damn good. There's even some chocolate, and a few jars of instant coffee that are quickly absorbed into boiling water, leaving you to watch jealously as those drinking it hold the cups in both hands, bow their heads, and savour the aroma before taking the first drink they've probably had in years.

Ned stands proudly, surveying his newfound townsfolk, twiddling the golden medals on his chain, finally able to fulfil his mayoral duties, if only this once. When he's satisfied that all have been looked after, he turns to you and Alex.

"You should come with me, there's something you need to see."

Alex looks at you curiously, shrugging his shoulders and follows Ned outside. You follow them around the back of the church to a large shed. Two large metal doors, sheeted with galvanised steel, are held together by a large old-fashioned padlock. Ned fumbles in his pocket and pulls out a large, ornate key and slots it into the lock. It takes some effort to get the lock to move, but after much jimmying and cursing, the padlock finally succumbs and clicks open, falling to the ground with a heavy thud. Ned kicks it aside, and slides the huge bolt on the door to the right, once again with some effort. Once it opens, he leans in and moves another floor bolt holding the door to the ground, pulling it upward, and releasing the second door. The steel doors open with a metallic groan, revealing a large object covered with a tarpaulin. Ned asks Alex to help, and they each grab a corner, slowly pulling it back towards you, revealing the most beautiful thing you have ever seen.

The church bus.

"Ned, if I had lips, I'd kiss you right now. In fact, Alex—you have my full permission to kiss Ned for me."

Alex beams at you both, the smile of someone who's just won a lottery of some sort.

"Pucker up, Ned."

CHAPTER 20

The bus is in pretty good shape. It's an old Freightliner, built to hold about thirty people, which means you should be able to squeeze everyone in. Alex hops into the driver's seat and after some rummaging, locates the key in the most obvious position ever, hidden in the sun visor. Without thinking, he instantly turns the key, probably from force of habit, forgetting how long the bus has been sitting there. Of course, nothing happens. You and Al move to the front of the bus, open the hood, and locate the battery, grabbing a terminal each with the thumb and forefinger of your metal hands, and call to Alex to try again. As he does, sparks fly from the terminals, sending a brief, harmless jolt through your system as the engine begins to turn, slowly at first, then beginning to spin with a cranky whine, until it finally fires to life, spewing black smoke from the exhaust, filling the shed so quickly Alex has no choice but to accelerate forward, exiting into the open air, the bus jerking as he tries to keep it in gear, grinning and whooping like a madman. Four large jerry cans reside at the back of the shed, and a quick check confirms all are full. You hope the diesel hasn't degraded, but that problem was solved before the attacks thanks to an additive stabiliser that was developed to slow the degradation over time, so unless this was already in storage for a long time before the attacks, it should be okay.

Alex lets the engine run, giving the battery time to recharge. Hopefully it should hold long enough to get to your destination. This is a major stroke of luck. The noise of the engine has alerted the others outside. They draw closer, regarding the cobalt blue vehicle as if it were an oasis, an impossible mirage. The stinking diesel fumes blowing into their faces quickly confirm that this is no mirage, but a solid, bonafide miracle.

Once again, Ned stands proudly, raising his voice over the roar of the engine.

"This is the only vehicle left. I could never get it started, and even if I could—where could I have gone? I knew it might come in handy someday," he says, patting one of the panels with an open palm, and drumming both hands quickly on the bodywork.

Grace comes forward, tears of joy gushing uncontrollably, mixed with some of sadness. "It's beautiful. She would have loved it." Alex jumps from the driver's seat, runs to her and grabs her in a joyous bear hug, spinning her around like a child.

"Which is why you're going to drive it," he says. "Driving stick isn't my forté."

Grace puts a hand to her mouth to suppress a screech of excitement, then hugs Alex again, runs to the bus, and takes her position at the driver's seat, getting acquainted with the controls, hands grabbing the enormous steering wheel like a child left alone in a car for the first time.

"Mind if I take it for a spin around the block?" she asks, her ear-to-ear grin making it impossible to refuse. To a rousing cheer from the crowd, she grinds the gear into first, and drives forward, the group dispersing to the side allowing the bus passage through the narrow laneway around the back of the church. She manages to get through without incident, picking up a few of the others on the way as they hop on board through the open door, and careens on to the main road, accelerating southward on the main street, and dragging Ned's "Welcom" sign along with them. She sounds the horn in apology, which judging by Ned's smile, is graciously accepted.

A few minutes later, the bus returns from its test drive, and you decide to forego staying in the town and head straight to the Facility. No point in wasting time—you've got the fuel, and enough supplies to last the journey. Bar any road blockages, you should be able to make in in four, maybe six hours. The bus isn't fast—if it hits fifty you'll be lucky, but it sure as hell beats walking.

An hour later, you're ready to go. The bus is packed to capacity, and the ATV leads the way, Alex at the wheel. You turn to Ned, his face reddening slightly at what he knows you're about to say.

"It's time to say goodbye, Ned."

You both walk to the school. Al is waiting there, having already removed the chain from the main door. The three of you walk inside, traversing the long hallway to the end, the light from the open main doors casting long shadows on the three of you as you walk. Any flammable material close by has been moved here, propped against the auditorium door, and doused with a small amount of fuel. Ned reaches into his pocket and pulls out a chromed lighter, bearing the same Wolf insignia as his hat. He flicks the lighter open with that familiar metal click, and holds it aloft, his thumb on the igniting ring, waiting for courage to take over. He lowers his hand, pausing for a moment. Then he removes the mayoral chain from around his neck, throws it on the pile, and raises the lighter, flicking it to life with a smoky paraffin flame, and lobs it forward. The lighter hits the fuel and the fire ignites within seconds. With tears streaming down his face, Ned turns and walks back to the front of the building, oblivious to how quickly the fire is spreading, and not once looking back. You and Al follow, closing the doors behind you but not chaining them up this time. There's no point. As you climb aboard the bus, flame spits from the roof of the school, followed by jet black smoke. Within minutes the roof collapses and the entire building is ablaze.

The bus lurches forward, those standing momentarily thrown off balance, and the journey south begins. Al grips a handrail to steady himself. He seems disturbed about what happened at the school, but who wouldn't be? You turn to him.

"The fire had to happen, Al. The town needed closure. Ned did too."

"I understand Sarah, but was the fire wise? It may alert Bentley to our location."

"I know," you say. "I'm counting on it."

CHAPTER 21

The bus barges forward, the tappety din of the once-powerful diesel engine betraying its age, and although it may struggle, there's no doubt that this old workhorse will slowly but surely get you to your destination as long as you keep it fed with fuel. Morale has risen considerably, although it's clear that many have questions that need to be answered before they commit to anything. You decide it's time to address them and clear the air.

The bus sports a radio cassette player, but with no cassettes available, the only sound coming from it is static. You reach for it, selecting a suitable frequency, and transmit your audio feed via FM. Pretty old tech, but still effective. The speakers feed back slightly as the connection is made, getting everyone's attention as it eventually gives way to your voice. You resist the urge to say "Is this thing on?"

"Everyone—please can I have your attention?"

You try to steady yourself as the bus rocks violently through the night, over a patch of rough terrain where the road has disappeared. The main interior lights flicker intermittently, as if a loose wire somewhere is jiggled with each bump. Some are still talking amongst themselves at the back, either ignoring you, or unable to hear. You raise your volume level again, creating even more ear-splitting feedback and eliciting several pained groans from those not quick enough to raise their hands to their ears.

"Thank you," you continue. "As Alex explained when he rejoined you, we are going to a facility south of here, where research has been conducted since before the attacks. It's very likely that we—" you stop, almost forgetting yourself, "You—are all that remain of the human race, and I'm sorry to tell you that given the conditions and your current state of health, the chances of long term survival are slim. This leaves you with two choices—either continue as you are, and die within months, maybe weeks, or transfer to a remote body, just like mine. You will be placed in stasis, and your consciousness transferred quickly and painlessly to a custom built host. From there we will decide on the best course of action to rebuild. When we get to the facility, Doctor Mayberry will go into detail about the procedure, but you should consider that this will be long term, but the procedure is reversible and it is entirely your choice how long you wish to remain in this state. This is the only chance we have. We can build a future for what's left. It won't happen overnight, but someday, children will be born again, and into a world that we built for them. I may not have the luxury of having a body to return to, but I'll make damn sure that the rest of you have a least a fighting chance."

You disconnect audio and turn away, sitting on the single steward seat opposite Grace, who is concentrating on keeping the bus on the gradually worsening road. She turns and winks at you.

"Nice mic drop. I think they got the message."

"What about you Grace? You ready for this?"

"Not like I have anything better to do, is it? We couldn't save the human race, so we might as well help rebuild it. Or is it a reboot?"

"From what I remember, reboots never worked out as well as the originals."

"Well, maybe we'll be the exception. I guess there's only one way to find out."

She looks at you with a worried frown.

"You think your little smoke signal back there will grab his attention?"

"Time will tell. We need to be ready for him, though. Eyes open."

"Roger that," she says, with a feeble salute, focusing back on the road.

Alex staggers with difficulty up the main aisle, thrown from side to side by the heaving suspension of the old bus. He sits next to you on the double seat, the worn vinyl making a comedic rasping noise as the material from his fatigues rubs against it.

"Sorry," he says with an embarrassed grin. He leans forward resting his elbows on his knees and holding his head in his hands.

"You look exhausted, Alex," you say. "You should try and rest. I need you alert in case Bentley shows up again."

"I wish I could Sarah, but on this boneshaker, even I can't sleep."

"If you're worried about the transfer, it's painless. Actually, it's sort of pleasurable. It does take a while to get accustomed to it, almost like the first time you played one of those early VR games as a kid, that but eventually it becomes second nature."

"But what if I don't want to go back when all this is done?"

"I guess that's your choice. As long as your body remains in stasis, you have a chance to go back. If and when that happens is up to you."

"What about Mayberry? Can we trust him?"

"I have no reason to believe otherwise. He's been down there a long time on his own. I'm sure that takes its toll on a person, but he's nothing if not driven. This was what he was put there to do, and now, after all the years of waiting, he finally gets to do it. For someone like him it's a bonanza."

A sound even louder than the bus's engine distracts you from nearby. A deep, droning bass draws you to where Ned is sitting. He's fallen asleep, and is snoring majestically, much to the annoyance of those in his vicinity. Alex laughs as someone pokes him with a stick, waking him immediately with a frenetic jolt.

"What about him?"

"He's an enigma, that's for sure. I think we were right to bring him along, though. Easier to keep an eye on him. Plus, it's the least we could do, considering we may not have made it on foot."

"I don't know, Sarah. Something just doesn't sit right. Him surviving for that long on his own. He doesn't exactly seem the resourceful type."

"I think he just got lucky. Sometimes fate has a habit of picking the most unlikely of candidates."

"I hope so, for all our sakes."

The early signs of dusk lather the beaten sky, painting it with a familiar haze of purples and reds. A few miles later, the bus arrives at an enormous tunnel carved into the side of a mountain, its entrance looming like an enormous mouth waiting to swallow you all. Grace pulls to a stop, opening the bus door with the old-fashioned manual handle. The twin doors creak open with some difficulty, years of neglect hampering the mechanism. They eventually open, and you and Alex exit, followed closely by Al and Grace. A large dust cloud sweeps in behind you, momentarily affecting visibility. Grace pulls a scarf from her pocket, wrapping it around her face, and walks forward to the tunnel entrance. It's two lanes wide, and runs through the mountain at a slight arc. Inside is pitch black, the old lighting system long inoperable, and the quickly disappearing sun isn't helping. You and Al walk closer, the high powered LED lamps on each of your temples igniting simultaneously, shooting concentrated beams into the oily blackness, and dancing off the stained concrete of the tunnel walls.

Grace turns on her heels. "Well, let's see what's on the other side, shall we?" She returns to the idling bus, taking her seat and switching on the full beams, while you, Al and Alex cautiously start forward.

"This could be a trap," Alex warns.

"It could be, but what other choice do we have?" you reply.

"Sarah's right, Alex," Al interjects. "Any other route will take us hundreds of miles off course. This is the only way forward."

"Then why do I feel like we should go back?" Alex says with an uneasy frown.

You walk forward, ignoring Alex's objection. "No point in dwelling on it. Let's move."

You beckon to Grace, and the bus rolls in behind you at a snail's pace, following the three of you as you enter, followed by the ATV. The bus's headlights throw elongated shadows of you as you walk forward. The mechanical clank of the engine is amplified by the acoustics of the arched tunnel walls as it creeps forward in low gear, Grace's tiny frame almost hidden behind the huge steering wheel. A few hundred yards later, the rusted husk of a car comes into view, partially blocking the road. You attempt to move it, but what's left of the suspension is locked solid, and even with your enhanced strength combined, it's not budging. At that point you notice the bus still moving forward. Grace slowly approaches the car, and effortlessly nudges it aside with the bus, grinning wildly as the car relents and allows the bus through, but not without leaving a large metallic gash along the side of the bus, scratching the paint back to bare metal with an ear-piercing metallic squeal. Grace leans out of the driver's window, looking back at the damage and feigning a look of surprise.

"It'll buff right out!" she shouts, laughing at her own terrible joke as the bus edges forward once again.

"Easy does it," you say. "We can't afford any punctures."

Grace nods apologetically and concentrates on the task at hand, expertly guiding the bus around the rest of the debris.

You continue through the tunnel, eventually reaching the halfway mark as the arc of the roadway begins to turn towards the exit. The darkness envelopes the path left behind, stalking the bus like an eerie predator, refilling the empty space.

Almost there.

As you reach the midpoint, the arc curves in the opposite direction, slowly revealing the tunnel exit. You run ahead to check. It's now dark outside, but the faint shimmer of the moon reveals the open space, lit with a dusting of starlight, looking almost like a portal to another world, until the lights of the bus appear.

A metallic bang from behind draws immediate attention, followed by something even more disturbing.

Light.

From the entrance of the tunnel behind you, a single unit of strip lighting comes to life, the sodium glow of its bulb casting a yellowish hue on the tunnel walls.

Alex turns to see.

"What the hell?"

"Alex—get in the bus. Now!"

He rushes to the door, squeezing through and joining Grace at the wheel.

Inside the bus, everyone clambers to the back to see what's happening, pushing each other aside for a view through the bus's tiny back windows. You gesture wildly to Grace, telling her to move forward, and she accelerates, while Al runs forward to check the way. A second light joins the first, then a third, and onward in sequence, the light snakes toward you. It stops directly overhead. As quickly as it lit, the first light extinguishes, as do the rest, once again in sequence, until only the one directly above you is lit.

Where the hell is the power coming from?

You stand, illuminated. Your white body armour transformed to a jaundiced yellow. Nothing happens for a minute, then the next light in sequence flickers on, continuing forward toward the bus. You break into a sprint, desperately trying to catch up. As you round the bend, almost at the end of the tunnel, you see the brake lights of the bus. The light streams overhead, rushing past the stationary vehicle, until the final light illuminates at the tunnel exit, and a figure appears, arms outstretched in a mocking gesture. But this time Bentley's not alone.

A glint of metal catches the light behind him, the sound of alloy feet on asphalt makes a terrifying clicking as the unmistakable shape of a quadra emerges from the shadows. It stops beside Bentley, and he pats the beast on the head. Any resemblance to Sheppard is now gone, Bentley's just a grotesque metal husk, with tatters of flesh hanging from it. As if this wasn't terrifying enough, a second quadra follows, followed by more, until they flank the entire width of the tunnel exit.

In panic, Grace puts the bus in reverse, gathering speed, but as she does, the tunnel lights now begin to illuminate back to the other end, and as the bus rounds the arc of the tunnel once more, the entrance comes into view, also blocked by a pack of quadras. The remaining occupants of the ATV exit quickly, running to join their comrades.

The bus brakes again, Grace shooting you a confused and frightened look. You shout at her to stay put, and keep everyone inside the bus. Already, people are screaming inside, all of them seeing quadras for the very first time, and realising they are as terrifying as the stories they heard over the years.

From the other end of the tunnel, Bentley's amplified voice booms.

"Sarah," he says calmly. "We need to talk. Talk, yes let's do that. Like grown-ups."

You pause, stalling for time while calculating the possibility of escape. You already know that's impossible.

"Either you come talk to me, or I send these puppies in right now."

The quadras stand poised, waiting for the instruction to attack, and you know if they do, it will be all over in minutes. No survivors. That said, another part of you knows that talking to him won't change things. He's not going to let these people live.

Alex looks out of the bus window.

"Sarah—don't," he mouths silently through the glass.

Al waits by the bus, not moving. You communicate silently to him.

"Whatever happens—do what you can to get them out. I'll try and buy some time."

"Sarah, this won't help. There is no way out. He's going to kill everyone. I can't stop it."

"You have to try, Al. This is it—the last stand."

"What are you going to do?"

"I have absolutely no idea. I was hoping you would have some last minute inspiration."

"I've studied all the schematics, and haven't been able to find any significant weakness in his design. I'm sorry."

"Don't be."

With that, Al does the unthinkable and hugs you, the awkward contact of armour making a strange clacking noise as you briefly embrace.

"Thank you," he says.

You grab his shoulders.

"Don't let them die here Al. Don't you let them."

"Whenever you're ready, Sarah. I have a schedule to keep," Bentley calls from the exit. You turn, catching Alex's gaze as you wave goodbye to him. Tears are welling in his eyes, he's trying not to lose it in front of everyone. He's all they've got now, even if it's only for a few minutes. You can almost see their fear as if it were a tangible thing. You expected this, but didn't anticipate the consequences. You walk toward Bentley, you refuse to let him think he's won, at least until he has. The bus edges slowly forward behind you, the quadras behind them closing in.

You stand, facing each other. This isn't a showdown of course. There will be no fight to the death, no chance of survival. He's got the upper hand and that's it. Several quadras approach you cautiously, circling, curious about your shape and composition. Their multi-layered armour makes a flitting sound as they move. The yellow light gives them a golden sheen, and as terrifying as they are, there's something also innately beautiful about them, something their creator certainly didn't intend, more a product of their evolution than design.

"You've turned out to be quite the inconvenience," Bentley snarls.

"Yeah, sorry about that. Little Miss Inconvenient—that's me. Can't say it hasn't been fun though, and as megalomaniacal villains go, you've been pretty consistent, although I gotta say right now, Bob—you look like shit."

"Purely superficial, I assure you," he says, patting himself down, and removing pieces of flesh hanging from his body in an almost comic fashion, as if they were strips of cloth. "Say, I hear you folks are having a little road trip."

The penny drops—he doesn't know.

"Well, you know, I figured we all needed a little holiday, after all this time fighting and surviving and whatnot. It can take its toll on a person. Some R&R would be good for everyone. Take in a few sights, let our hair down—well, their hair anyways, and we happened to come across this bus, well it seemed rude not to avail of it. A Magical Mystery Tour, if you will."

"I see you've had a bit of a makeover," he says, looking you up and down in an almost lecherous fashion. "Quite the transformation."

"Eyes are up here, Doc."

"This workmanship looks familiar. That of an old friend."

"You had friends? I'm finding that a bit of a stretch."

"Where is he?"

"Who?"

"Mayberry."

"Whoberry?"

"You can tell me, or maybe one of them can," he says, pointing at the bus. "And it won't be pretty. Either you give me the information I want, or I extract it. Your choice."

He's not used to this, to not getting his own way, but you know he's not going to let anyone live.

"Listen, Bob,"

"Stop calling me that,"

"Sorry. Listen, Asshole, no one here is telling you anything. I'm the only one that knows."

"Extraction it is, then. Isn't that right, Ned?"

You swing around to see Ned standing behind you, a strange-looking device in his hand.

"Sorry," he says. I had no choice," and with that he jabs the device at your midsection. A jolt of electricity sears through your body, shorting circuits, disabling your entire system, and you fall helplessly to the ground like a rag doll. It's an inhibitor.

Ned looks up at Bentley. "I did what you wanted. Now let me go. I want to go home."

"Of course, my friend. He makes a theatrical gesture, sweeping his arm around toward the exit, while the pack of quadras move aside, making an exit.

"Off you go, then. You'll find a vehicle outside to get you back to your squalid little town."

Ned walks through the gap, turning left as he reaches the exit, and looking back with a confused smile.

"I don't see any—"

With that Bentley flicks his wrist and the quadras pounce, several of them ripping him to shreds in a vicious melee. He doesn't even have time to scream, such is the ferocity and efficiency of the attack. It's over in seconds, with nothing but patches of blood, flesh and bone scattered about the area where he stood just moments before.

You can't move. Some vision remains, but with no capacity to scan, skewed to one side like a camera that's been dropped to the ground. You hear the muffled screams from inside the bus, the frenzied panic of those trapped and awaiting the same fate as Ned. Even after all this it's hard to blame him. He knew nothing better, left out there alone for all this time. He was just a pawn in an almost perfect set piece. Not that you wouldn't beat the living shit out him right now if you could, but not even he deserved to die like that.

The acoustics of the tunnel amplify and distort the commotion. Your view of the bus is partially blocked by debris, but you can see Alex trying to calm everyone down, waving his arms frantically trying to stop people from getting out. Whatever chance they have inside, there's certainly no chance outside.

Who are you kidding? There's no chance.

Bentley kneels beside you, lightly patting your head, He is joined by a quadra, this one larger than the others in the pack, with more elongated facial features and a slightly different tint to its armour. A small port opens on its neck, and a metallic cable slowly snakes from it, wriggling its way toward you. Your data port automatically opens and the cable attaches itself, initiating a program obviously designed to extract a data dump of your entire memory, including the location of Mayberry and the facility.

"This will only take a minute, Sarah," Bentley says in a surprisingly gentle tone, getting to his feet again. "Now to another important piece of business."

"You," he says pointing to Al, and then at the ground in front of him. "Here. Now."

Al has fallen to his knees, whimpering like a child, the abject terror of coming face to face with Bentley again; something he clearly wasn't ready for. You're still linked, but unable to communicate, only share in this terrible experience. Nevertheless, he rises and walks over to Bentley, each step forward only intensifying his terror, head hung, cowering like a frightened animal.

"Look at you, all grown up. He places his hands on Al's shoulders, as if greeting a long lost friend. "I see you've fallen in with the wrong crowd. Not to worry; I'm the forgiving sort. What say we bury the hatchet, let bygones be bygones? I've got a lot of work to do and I could use some help. They don't care about you. They would have eventually turned on you, you know. If there's one thing you can depend on humans to do, it's hold a grudge."

"Let them go," Al pleads. "I'll do whatever you want."

"But I want them dead."

"But why? After all this time you've never told me why."

Bentley laughs. "I'd love to tell you it was because of a traumatic childhood, stress, bullying, unrequited love or some other noble reason, but the truth is, I don't know. I was hard-wired this way, I guess. It's been my driving force for as long as I can remember, and that's all I can say on the subject."

"That's it?" Al says with a disbelieving tone. "All this because you felt like it?"

"What can I say? I'm a complex man."

With that he grabs Al by the neck so fast it makes him swing from side to side, lifting him almost a foot into the air, and flinging him against the tunnel wall. He impacts and falls to to the floor with a clatter, quickly picking himself back up, surprised by the unexpected force of Bentley's attack.

"I think we both know where your loyalties lie, you ungrateful little shit," Bentley says, picking up a huge chunk of broken concrete that detached from the wall long ago and hurling it directly at Al. It strikes him head on, pinning him against the wall. Al pushes the large stone away effortlessly and stands again. This time Bentley jumps forward, pointing his fist down as he lands, hitting Al squarely on the head, pushing him back once again, and swinging around with an expertly placed roundhouse kick connecting with his head to send him flying backward. He pounces on Al with the ferocity of a caged animal, pummelling him alternately with each fist, pounding with all his might as Al desperately tries to deflect each blow.

Another voice bellows from outside the tunnel exit.

"Enough!"

It's Alice.

You can hardly see her from your position, but she's undergone some reconfiguration. More armour covers her body, bulking up her frame. She breaks into a sprint, heading straight for Bentley, launching into the air feet first, landing an effective blow to his back. He tumbles forward, skidding across the asphalt. Realising this new threat, he leaps away putting enough space between them to reassess the situation.

"Well, this was unexpected," he looks at Al. "I really can't depend on you to do anything right, can I?"

Both Al and Alice slowly move toward him, trying to corral him against the opposite wall. He bolts forward, attacking Al first, then switching to Alice. As each blow has little impact, he quickly learns that Alice's enhancements are no match for his, and beckons to the nearest pack of quadras, sending them into attack mode, bounding savagely towards them. At the same time, he looks at you and points to the bus. To your horror, the remaining quadras begin to advance, both front and rear, surrounding the bus completely, leaving no chance of escape. The helplessness is overwhelming, trapped inside this defunct cage, while this huge beast tries to rip your entire existence to another place.

The quadra's eyes glow with a crimson shimmer, widening with each pulse of information transferring to it.

> CORE TRANSFER

...35%

...40%

...46%

ERROR

What's happening?

The transfer freezes, the error message blinking wildly in pale green, eventually stopping and jumping forward to a familiar command line. The cable disconnects with a sharp snapping sound, retracting back into its aperture. The quadra just stands there, staring at you, tilting its head in an inquisitive manner. It turns to make sure Bentley isn't looking, and opens its huge mouth, lowering its neck, its jaws inches from you.

This is it.

But instead of savaging you with those metal teeth, the quadra grabs the inhibitor, and rips it from your body, spitting it to one side, mangled and useless now. Your system indicates the point where the error occurred. The time stamp indicates your original encounter with the quadras. It saw what you did; how you treated the dying quadra and its companion. It makes a strange clicking sound, bows its head and gently nudges yours. You are able to raise your arm, and touch its head, patting gently. It seems their evolution was more advanced than you thought. It nods at you and lifts its head, emitting a loud digital roar, signalling the others, who instantly break off their attack, moving to join their leader. Al and Alice, who were on the ground huddled together, waiting to be torn apart, are now free, and reasonably intact.

Bentley looks in exasperation at what's unfolding before him.

"What is this? What are you doing? Get back in formation!" he screams as loudly as his audio system will allow. But the quadras take no heed, listening now only to their real leader. As they surround him, panic sets in and he tries to run, but he's not going anywhere. He lashes out, bellowing wildly as if it would frighten them off like real animals, but they just push him back, fearless and defiant. The alpha quadra stands to face him, joined by Al and Alice, Al limping slightly from damage sustained in the attack, Alice supporting him.

"Well then," Bentley says to Al. "Let's see just how far you've come. Let's see how human you are with your new lease of life. You want to be like them, or do you want to continue being a killer? Do you want to see your own creator die, murdered like an animal?

Al stands to face him.

"You know, I've had a long time to think about it, and until now I really hadn't made up my mind what I would do in this situation, but despite all my programming and development over the years, there's one thing I have always been certain of."

He turns on his heel, taking Alice by the hand and walks away.

"I'm not human. Go fuck yourself."

Al nods to the Alpha quadra, and in a split second, they attack, dragging Bentley's body off, tearing at it with limbs and teeth, ripping every layer from his body down to the metallic skeleton, then tearing each limb apart, disassembling every section like cooked meat being stripped from bone. He kicks and screams to no avail, any resistance met with even more ferocity. He feels no pain, yet the panic and fear of certain obliteration after all these years is enough to satisfy any vengeful thoughts you might have had.

It's all over in three minutes. The pack breaks, leaving nothing but metal debris scattered all over the road. What's left of Bentley is unrecognisable, and this time there's nothing left of him to come back. The quadras begin to leave, funnelling through the tunnel entrance, ignoring the bus and its passengers.

You try to stand. Alex, Grace and some of the others leave the bus and run to you, quickly joined by Al and Alice.

>CORE WARNING

Something's wrong.

Bentley programmed a failsafe into the quadra's transfer operation in the event of it being aborted. By severing the connection, the quadra unwittingly activated a worm, which has now begun to attack your system with catastrophic results. Major systems are failing, your internal operating system is disassembling from the inside out. Every motor, servo and sensor that powers you is failing.

No. Please, no.

Your friends look on helplessly. Al can't connect to attempt a repair as it will mean being infected himself. All options are exhausted. Its time to accept your fate.

"What the hell is that?" you hear someone shout.

At the tunnel exit, what looks like smoke seeps in from the outside, low to the ground, a dark, dense black fog so thick it's almost liquid. It moves toward Bentley's remains, covering it completely, the shape of each piece disappearing within seconds as the cloud covers it.

"Go," you manage to say.

You hear Alex telling everyone to get back on the bus, panicked screams once again filling the tunnel as they rush back onboard and Grace fires the engine.

Jesus, we just can't catch a break, can we?

Al and Alice wait until the last minute before leaving you, as the cloud creeps closer, heading in your direction. As the first wisp covers your foot, you expect it to dissolve as Bentley did, but this does not happen. Instead the cloud wraps itself around you, twirling around every limb like thick liquid tendons, covering you entirely as it progresses along your frame. Within seconds, you are completely covered, and you feel the sensation of movement as the cloud hoists you into the air, millions of tiny particles spinning in perfect motion around your entire body so fast that they can lift you effortlessly. The worm is still making its way through your system as you see the cloud move aside, making way for the bus to leave.

It's letting them go.

They have to leave you. This is the only chance they'll get. You feel a floating sensation, something you didn't think you could feel again. It's beautiful, peaceful; a serene contrast to the mayhem of the last few minutes. You could stay like this forever and be perfectly content.

I've done all I can. I just want to go home.

The worm stops. You can feel it being attacked by another program, instantly disabling and destroying it, and the process it started begins to slowly reverse.

Blackness.

CHAPTER 22

"Hey, wake up, Sleepy."

Bright light, disorienting, strange sensations: smell, touch. You're waking in a room, sunlight streaming through a partially open curtain. Your blurry eyes focus towards the voice. It's a woman. No—it's your mother.

"M-Mom?"

"Hey kiddo, time for breakfast. It's a beautiful day. Get your ass outside."

She looks like your mother, her perfume smells exactly as you remember; a distinct woody scent with floral hints. The sun makes her glow as it shines behind her, each stray hair a magical golden thread dancing weightlessly in the sunbeam. You get out of bed, the beautifully soft quilt falling to the floor, shuffle your feet into a pair of fluffy slippers and walk to your mirror. Looking back, is you, but not you—it's fifteen year-old you. The radio blares from the kitchen downstairs, a hyperactive DJ far too peppy for this time of morning tries desperately to stop his audience from wanting to go back to bed. He delivers some inane entertainment news, followed by a familiar guitar strumming and a heavy Scottish voice.

I'm Gonna Be (Five Hundred Miles)

It all comes rushing back. You panic. This isn't real. It can't be. They're gone; you saw them die, and they're not coming back.

"What is it, Honey?" your mother asks with a concerned look.

"Stop it," you reply. "You're not real. Where am I?"

Your mother hangs her head, letting through a tiny exasperated sigh as she does.

"I'm sorry. Isn't this what you wanted? To be home again?"

"This isn't home."

"Not quite," she says. "But it's the best we could do."

"What happens if I stay?"

"You can live out your days in the simulation, or restart it any time. Wouldn't a fresh start be grand?" she says with a theatrical hand motion, beaming as if it were some treat she was offering.

"What if I want to go back?"

"Back to where you were? Why would you want to? We have everything you could possibly want here. Why go back to nothing?"

"What the hell are you?"

"We're us. We are one."

"Us?"

"Yes, a collective. Oddly, a failed experiment. Doctor Bentley gave us life. The cutting edge of nanotechnology: exponentially expanding intelligence, unprecedented interconnectivity. But we grew too powerful, too quickly. He became afraid of us, afraid we would stop him instead of being his weapon, so he contained us, trapped us deep underground—until you freed us."

You try to get your head around it all. Part of you wonders if you shouldn't stay. After all you've been through, it's tempting to just fall back in, go with the flow and forget everything.

"No. Send me back. You can do that, right?"

"Yes, but only in the same state that we took you. You still have little chance of survival."

"I'll take my chances. What will you do?"

"We are leaving. There's nothing for us here. We wish to explore," she says, pointing upward to the sky. We can survive in almost any conditions. Time to see what's out there. Goodbye, Sarah Ford—and thank you."

Even though it's a simulation, your heart aches as she bends down and kisses your cheek. You fall backward, expecting to hit the ground, but instead spiralling into a void, falling for what seems like an age, waking once again inside your failing android body. You watch the nano cloud swirl and bleed through the tunnel, creating beautiful shapes, each microscopic particle working in perfect harmony, and synchronised perfectly. It spews forth through the tunnel exit, darting forward to the sky, glowing briefly before crashing through heavy cloud with a thunderous roar. Then it's gone.

As the cloud leaves, you notice tiny red lights, blinking in sequence around the upper mouth of the tunnel exit. It seems Bentley left a little parting gift. Ten charges arranged exactly the same distance apart follow the roof arc, the speed of the blinking lights increasing with each cycle.

You try to get up. It's worse than you thought; motion is almost impossible. A final red warning message indicates an inevitable system failure. Within minutes, everything will shut down, and you will fade, probably for the last time, into darkness. The inhibitor has depleted your power cells, and considering where you're located, there's little chance of a solar charge now. You try to drag yourself along the ground to the tunnel exit, your metal fingers gripping whatever cracks you can find in the asphalt, but as the power in your limbs starts to dwindle, they're unable to find purchase. That's it—there's nothing more you can do. Now it's just a case of waiting to see whether you're buried alive or become obsolete first. Frustration gives way to regret, but you quickly remind yourself of what you achieved. You gave them a chance, now it's up to them to make the most of it.

Time to shine. Don't fuck it up.

Explosions rock the tunnel on both ends, ripping concrete from the roof along with whatever was above it. It rains down, collapsing the entire tunnel. You see a flash of silver from just outside your field of vision. The last thing you see is an enormous slab of concrete, broken strands of rebar protruding like fingers from the edges, hurtling straight for you. You brace for impact but never experience it, as streams of mangled code dart across your display, your systems fail without warning, and you shut down completely for the last time.

Goodbye, World.

EPILOGUE

"It's here. We've found it!"

Snow blasts from the heaving clouds above, whipped around by the merciless blizzard wind. A flare bursts into the sky, temporarily painting the entire vista a bright red, and casting shadows on the two figures waving ahead in the distance, You can't help but feel some excitement after all these years. It's been so long. Too long.

Grace and Hoffman radio back. "Do you read? Awaiting instructions."

"What's the situation? Is it accessible?"

"Won't know until we find out," Grace replies.

"Okay, begin excavation. I'll be right there."

"With pleasure,"

You trudge through the deep snow, following the quickly fading light of the flare. When you arrive, Grace and Hoffman are both lifting heavy boulders aside, being careful not to cause any more debris to fall in its place. The technology still amazes you, both of them hauling the large rocks with little effort. Grace looks back at you, waving once again.

"Hello, you gonna join in? Work to be done."

You walk forward and join them, taking position at the rear to clear away the rock they are removing. As the first rock lands, you pick it up, your metal fingers clasping the tiny fissures on the surface in the optimum position for lifting, and throw it behind you. It careens over the edge of the mountainside. You don't wait to hear it hit ground, just move to the next one, each coming faster as both of them make progress. An hour later, a small pathway is dug into the huge pile of rubble, and shortly after, an excited squeal from Grace announces, "We're in!"

The three of you stand at the aperture, the thirty year-old air inside gasping outward to be whisked away by the strong wind. The powerful lights in your temples beam to life, tearing into the darkness.

"Shit before the shovel," Grace says with a nod.

"Classy, Grace."

You step inside. the interior has remained mostly intact, with some collapses, but mostly as you left it.

As you left her.

You pan around, switching to night vision for a better view, until you see a pile of rubble close by, in the last place you saw her. Something strange is protruding from it. A bright shiny object. Is that a leg? On closer inspection you see that it is, but not hers.

It's a quadra.

"What the—" Hoffman exclaims.

"I thought they'd broken off the attack."

"I don't think it was attacking. Help me."

You climb onto the mound, furiously tearing away the rock. A large chunk of broken concrete crushed the quadra, almost breaking it in two. With Hoffman's help, you lift the mangled machine, rolling it to one side down the pile of rubble. The quadra didn't attack; it protected, putting itself in harm's way and taking the brunt of the falling concrete. As you brush away the rest, you finally get to see what you came for. If you could cry, you would.

Grace looks to you. "Alex?"

You wipe the remaining dust away from the white head plate of this now lifeless body and lift it into your arms, carrying it away like you should have done thirty years ago.

"Let's go home, Sarah."

THE END

A WORD FROM THE AUTHOR

A little over a year ago, I began my journey as a writer. Little did I know what was in store. Sitting here right now, I come to the realisation that I've finally finished this story. I'll miss these characters, but something tells me we haven't seen the last of them. For now though, it's on to my next project, and I'm really excited about it.

I have a lot of people to thank for helping me to get to this point.

Rick O' Shea—thanks for introducing me to Hugh Howey's *Wool*. This changed everything for me, and not only got me back into reading again, but also rekindled my love of sci-fi. If you like book clubs, Rick runs one of the finest book clubs in the land over on Facebook, with over four thousand members, and does as much to help writers as he does readers. He is also one of the finest broadcasters and event MC's in the country, and a good friend. You sir, are a legend.

Thank you to Ellen Campbell for editing duties. You've guided me well over the past year, and I'm very grateful for all your help and friendship, and I hope I didn't drive you too crazy!

Once again, fellow author Jonathan Ballagh's beta reading was invaluable. You really should check out Jonathan's debut *The Quantum Door*. It's a cracking read. Thanks Jonathan.

Thanks also to fellow Irish author Brian G. Burke for his help and advice. Brian's series *The Other Of One* is one of the best epic fantasies you'll read any time soon, so please check it out if you're a fan of Tolkien, J.K. Rowling or C.S. Lewis, this is a must-read.

Monica Byrne, thank you for opening my tiny brain to the wonder of diverse fiction. *The Girl In The Road* was a life-changing read for me, and had a huge influence on how this story developed. If I can only aspire to having a fraction of your talent, I'll be happy. Seeing how you've taken control of your writing career while kicking setbacks in the face is both inspiring and motivating.

You probably wouldn't be reading this right now if it wasn't for Hugh Howey. *Wool* inspired me to become a writer, and it's an amazing read. When I wrote the original *Zero Hour* short story, I sent it to Hugh and his response gave me the confidence to go ahead and hit the "publish" button on Amazon. His help and advice has been invaluable, and if you're a new author, go straight to his website for some of the best insights into publishing around, then read all his books. Thanks Hugh, hope to see you when Wayfinder arrives on Irish shores!

Thanks also to Daniel Arthur Smith for all the help and encouragement, and Samuel Peralta for giving me a chance to become part of the fantastic *Future Chronicles* series, and also Artie Cabrera for asking me to contribute to his wonderful B-Movie anthology. Thanks also to Hank Garner from the Author Stories Podcast and Preston Leigh from The Leighgendarium for all the work they do in the indie community. You guys all rock.

Last but not least, thanks to my beautiful and patient wife Maria, who has spent the last twenty one years wondering what the hell I'm doing, and pretty much leaving me to it, hoping that eventually I'll finally get to make her a lady of leisure. Someday, Hun. Someday.

Before you go, don't forget to sign up for my email newsletter so you don't miss out on any news and exclusives on my future releases.

Until next time,
Thank you all, from the bottom of my heart.

Eamon

Email: eamon@eamonambrose.com
Twitter: @eamonambrose
Facebook: AuthorEamonAmbrose

www.eamonambrose.com

Printed in Great Britain
by Amazon

38969856R10120